THE CHICAGO SYNCOPATOR

28 Aug 2014

To D and Judy:

How precious this almost forty years of friendship has become. Thank you for all of your kindnesses and support over the years. I am deeply grateful. You have given my life amazing richness.

Phil

The Chicago Syncopator

A Bohemian Kid Tells About His Life in Jazz

A Novel

Philip T. Nemec

THE CHICAGO SYNCOPATOR
A BOHEMIAN KID TELLS ABOUT HIS LIFE IN JAZZ

© 2014 by Philip T. Nemec. All rights reserved.

All rights reserved. No part of this publication may be reproduced or transmitted in any form or by any means, electronic or mechanical, including photocopy, recording, or any information storage and retrieval system, without permission in writing from the publisher.

Please contact the publisher for permission to make copies of any part of this work.

WINDY CITY PUBLISHERS
2118 Plum Grove Road #349
Rolling Meadows, IL 60008
www.windycitypublishers.com

Published in the United States of America

Library of Congress Control Number:
2014937871

ISBN:
978-1-941478-04-2

WINDY CITY PUBLISHERS
CHICAGO

Dedicated to Benjamin J. Nemec Jr.

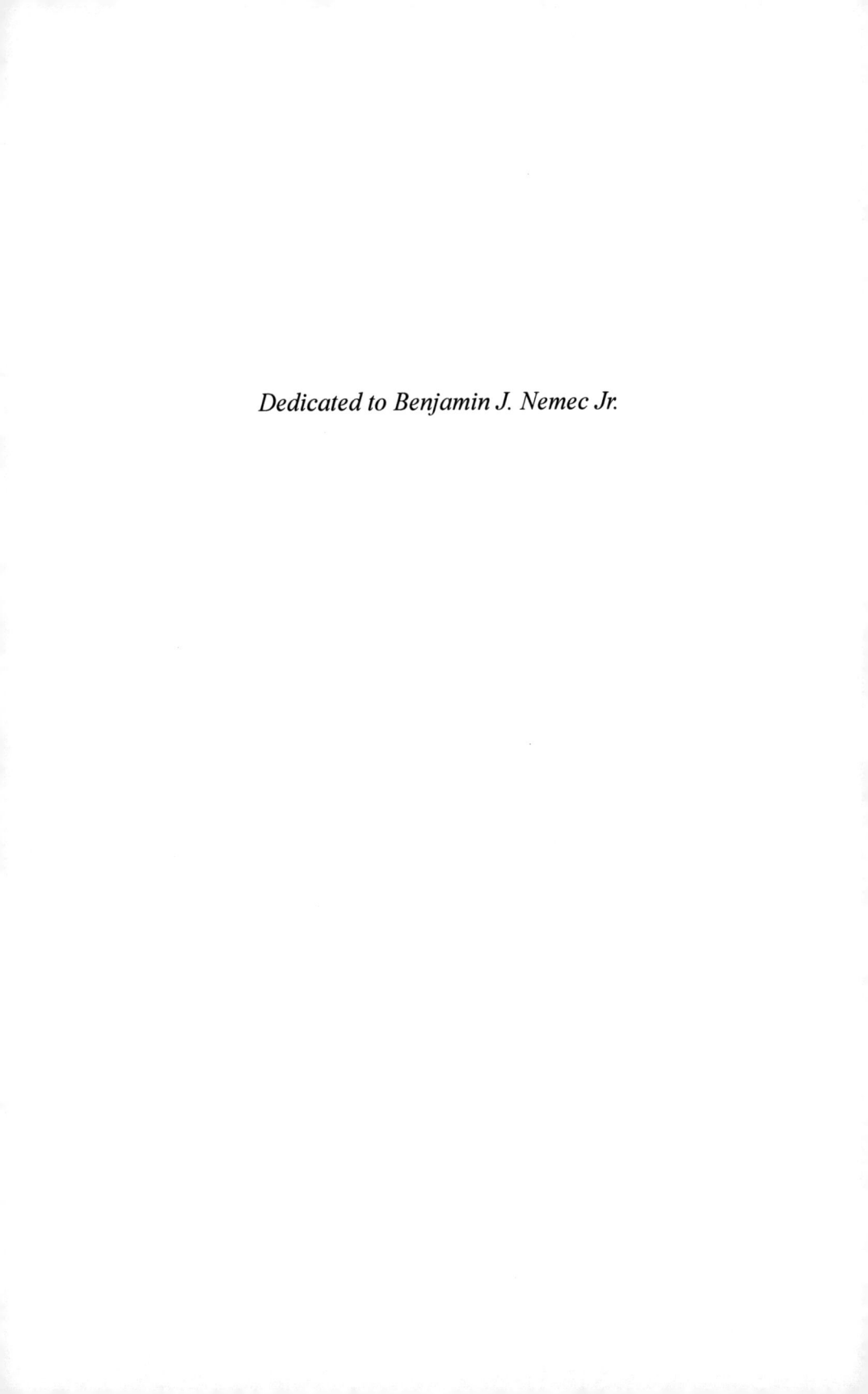

Acknowledgements

I'm grateful for the assistance, diligence, friendship, and patience my editor, D. M. DiSantis, has invested in this project.

Also, I would like express my appreciation to the loving memory of Charles M. Shelton, SJ of Regis University whose lifetime of support and advice has meant so much.

Syncopate

To displace the beats or accents in music or a rhythm so that strong beats become weak, and vice versa.

Beginning and Preface

My name is George Nepras, and I am a syncopator, a jazzman. I mark time by being offbeat. My beats make the weak ones strong and the strong ones weak. In my world I improvise. But the melody is always in the back of my head. Worked a lot of jobs, done a lot of things, failed more than once, and had the good fortune to be loved by a woman, but my life has been jazz. One day it landed on me like a tongue of fire that rested on my head till I spoke it in flame pouring out of my cornet and trumpet, and ever since it has lived banked in my heart. Next year, being 1961, will be the forty-second year my heart's been playing jazz.[1] But it don't seem like a long time. Jazz has changed over the years and so have I, and lately, I've begun to wonder if I'm supposed to be around for its next big change. That got me thinking I better tell my story now.

* * *

In spite of its syntax errors and overblown imagery, this opening to George Nepras's narrative grabbed me and led to my conviction that his manuscript deserved my effort. George's relationship with me began when he first visited my newspaper office almost two years ago, in 1962, wearing out of style sunglasses and carrying a hand-written manuscript proclaiming how it told the story of his life in jazz. Apparently, George had sought me out for no other reason than I was a journalist with a Czech, or as he would say, "Bohemian" family name. Though I explained that I was fully two generations removed from the "old country," he believed, nonetheless, that my name ordained me champion of his cause. I failed to dispel his belief that journalists possessed the power to dictate what publishing houses printed. Bluntly, I told him I had not a nickel's worth of interest in editing his work and even less interest in shepherding it to publication. Given my Czech roots, if I were attracted to any music it would be

Dvorak and Smetana, and not jazz, which I found at that time to be marginally entertaining and cacophonous.

George's persistence, despite my discouragement, led to several discussions. Some were pleasant and others were heated, especially as my frustration mounted over my inability to convince him that his manuscript was unworthy of publication. Admittedly, my emotions at the time were raw because of my own publication and byline struggles with my paper. Still, he kept coming back pursuing his self-declared mission to inspire young jazz musicians. I confess I don't know how much he was driven by obsession, voices in his head, or whether he was unaware of how many times he had visited. When he first appeared at my desk, my impression was that the years had taken their toll, making it difficult to estimate his age. If forced to guess at that time, I would have picked seventy. I recall the thought popping into my mind at our first meeting was that a shower and shave would have served his presentation better than the olfactory one he delivered.

With the likes of Miles Davis, John Coltrane, and Ornette Coleman currently fomenting a stir not only in jazz but the larger cultural world, jazz was topical. The intellectual question concerning this uniquely American art form of, "What is jazz?" was bubbling in the pot not unlike the controversy surrounding abstract painting. On the one hand, traditionalists were insisting that true jazz must mirror the form originally played in the Storyville District of New Orleans at the turn of the century. On the other hand, critics were viewing the work of modern musicians like trumpeter Miles Davis and his Kind of Blue *jazz LP, as offering a revolutionary and paradigm altering musical form. Though George was oblivious to this debate, his praise of Davis's music intrigued me and brought about a thawing in my unwillingness to take his manuscript seriously. This thaw, however, hardened into another ice age one bleak March day when George barged in without an appointment and reeking of garlic. I had several deadlines looming, was thoroughly fed up with the stresses of dealing with my shrew girlfriend, and was weary of George's rambling and circular entreaties which contained these annoying guttural stops and sing-song sentence endings that reminded me of my Aunt Violet. At that moment, I didn't give a damn about musicologists' drabble regarding paradigm shifts or anything else about jazz. In short, I had George chucked out of my office. I admit to some guilt, but it dissipated with time, and my life regained its normal, albeit frenetic, pace.*

Then one day more than a year ago, the mail clerk brought me a bundle wrapped in white bakery paper. Inside were the loose handwritten pages of George's manuscript, an envelope containing nearly a thousand dollars, and a letter instructing me to use the money to "work over" the manuscript and "get it made into a book." The letter went on to offer me all the profit from the book and said if, "some tycoon makes a movie out of it, you can keep that money too." I groaned.

I resolved to visit the return address that same day, hand back both money and manuscript, and once and for all persuade George to leave me in peace. To my chagrin, I learned that George had vanished. I felt bad the way most of us feel when we shove aside some character who unintentionally annoys us. The guilt I felt for my rudeness lingered. That, coupled with my journalistic instincts, drove me to investigate his whereabouts. Several stories circulated in his neighborhood about his disappearance. According to one neighbor, George announced he was departing on a Far East concert tour. He told another he was going off to play in the Paris jazz clubs. He'd asked one neighbor to collect his mail, but offered no details other than something about a "big engagement." He told her he'd be back in a week. One woman down the block swore she saw him leaving with a valise and cornet case. Chillingly, several rendered the opinion he had committed suicide, but were unable to offer any evidence to support that theory. The most typical response was a shrug of the shoulder.

George did not return. After two weeks, my hope truly faded. I must admit, suicide seemed more plausible with each passing day. My experience with him convinced me that it was absurd to entertain the notion he was playing the Paris scene or touring the Far East. Beyond beating myself up over my rudeness, I also had legal and ethical concerns about holding his money. Maybe he had simply gone somewhere, become disoriented or lost, and needed money; so I used some of the cash to hire a private investigator, to no avail. Toward the end of the manuscript George hinted about going to New Orleans, but the private dick uncovered no clues there.

With the assistance of the police and a cooperative neighbor who had a key, I entered George's home. He had left what appeared to be all of his possessions except for his cornet. Breakfast dishes were still in the sink; the bathroom light was on. A record search revealed that the deed to the house remained in his name, and he owned it free and clear. There were no known relatives. The Musician's Union was unhelpful. Ultimately, the police all but yawned in my face, and several months passed without a clue.

In our conversations I had been struck by how George believed he had succeeded and become a "jazzman." Was he delusional? Perhaps. But whose judgment of one's self-worth and success isn't at least in part delusional. Furthermore, how do we know what, if anything, will live on after we are gone? Time, events, myths, serendipity and so much more shape what survives and is remembered or at times venerated. How can we really know the future importance of life lived in the here and now?

For what it's worth, I don't even know what definition of success George used. Did he mean the brilliant jazz successes of the likes of Billie Holiday and Charlie Parker, whose lives were hobbled by drugs, or was there something else he was addressing? The most I can conclude is George seemed moved by some spiritual ideal, which he fervently hoped to pass on to young musicians. As I worked with his manuscript, I gradually understood its powerful moral and ethical message and came to appreciate how many of his values appear self-taught.

George had always maintained that he planned to "step off stage" when he felt the moment was right for younger musicians to take his place. He knew how tough the odds were at making it in music, and in his typically humble and self-effacing way, he wanted to share success. Despite the cold world that was his all-too-frequent accompanist, he somehow nurtured a spirit that fueled his desire to bequeath the goodness in his calling to a younger generation. In any event, whether he is alive or dead, George's manuscript is, in a sense, a last will and testament. It does not dispose of his property, but it does impart the secrets of his heart; and his heart's inner workings were obviously important to him. Where he is or what happened to him remains a mystery about which we are all welcome to conjecture.

At some point, and I'm not sure when, I decided the right thing to do was to work on the manuscript. I worried that if the taxes weren't paid, and the house wasn't maintained, the state might seize it. I reasoned that if I could salvage something of the manuscript it could provide a nest egg for him if he indeed lost everything else and one day resurfaced on my doorstep. At first, my goal was to do a human-interest piece built around his reminiscences. As I focused on that,

I gradually became entangled in his story. I interviewed neighbors. I researched some of the jazz legends he writes about like Bix Beiderbecke. Some of his experiences I was able to corroborate. Ultimately, however, further work on the human-interest piece proved dissatisfying. The story wasn't alive. That's when it dawned on me that what I needed to do was let George tell it. My job was to merely untangle his prose so the reader could absorb its message.

Based on my results, I couldn't think of a reason why his story shouldn't be told. In the final analysis George was, no that's wrong, is part of America's jazz history. Benny Goodman's and Duke Ellington's stories have already been written. In my research, I've found the autobiographies of jazz greats Eddie Condon and Sydney Bechet. Jazz clarinetist Mezz Mezzrow's autobiography, Really the Blues, *parallels George's musical beginnings in Chicago. In fact, they converge at one point. To be sure, some stories of jazz greats are little more than hagiographies. Why not let this man, whose parents journeyed from Prague rather than New Orleans, tell his version of a life in jazz? George's story, like the stories of other jazz musicians, is an American story. And since I am a Czech-American, I welcomed the opportunity to show how our common heritage became a unique piece of America's larger jazz story.*

In guiding his manuscript to publication, I hope I have been a good steward. I have changed as little as possible, largely sparing his syntax and diction. The title, paragraphing (George used none), chapter titles, and the definition of "to syncopate" are my revisions. I edited out some digressions that I found not germane. George records various conversations that I have placed in quotation marks. I obviously cannot authenticate their accuracy and must rely on George's memory for their truthfulness. Above all, more than anything, my goal was to ensure the story remains George's narrative.

George frequently mentions historical events. At times, he mistakes facts and dates. Rather than correcting George, I have chosen to footnote the historical references both to correct inaccuracies and to help amplify his narrative. I have translated various Czech words, and footnoted or defined uncommon phrases, references to places, and Bohemian foods,

It is unclear to me how long it took George to write his manuscript. At one point he told me he had taken his "whole life to write it," but quite possibly he was speaking figuratively. My observation of his handwritten manuscript—since he apparently uses the same type of paper, pen, and ink, (I could see where the pen's reservoir was periodically running dry and where he refilled it.) is that it could have been drafted in one session. Nevertheless, I detect changes in comprehension of the world around him between the first half and second half of the manuscript. It suggests to me that he might have been transcribing notes taken throughout his life. Again, the reader is free to speculate.

As I have found so often in life, the process or journey of doing something, even something that at first poses difficulties and setbacks, concludes with rewards one never anticipated. This has been true in this project as well. I have come to know and appreciate jazz, and in so doing, have come to better understand my own heart.

Not least of all, I have learned to appreciate the odyssey my grandparents took from Prague to Chicago in the late 19th century. To my surprise, I discovered that their first home in America was only a few blocks from George's first home in Chicago's Pilsen district. I can't help but wonder if they knew George's parents or maybe even George himself. If for no other reason, I am grateful for the insights his manuscript provided. I hope George would concur with my desire to dedicate this work not only to young "jazzmen," but also to those men and women who journeyed from Bohemia to Chicago and whose music syncopated to the rhythms of their new home. I sincerely hope George's manuscript captures you as much as it did me.

Charles Svoboda
Chicago 1964

Chapter 1

Thinking About My Life

George Nepras is a Bohemian[2] name. My Ma and Pa came from Prague, but my Ma's family originally came from Krumlov south of Budejovice. I've been told there's a castle there. The family lost contact with the old country. I don't know what else they lost by coming to America, but I've learned there are losses in everything you do. They were young when they came to Chicago. They came for the jobs, but Pa's first job was as a strikebreaker at the McCormick Reaper plant.[3] Bohemians fought Bohemians there, right in the old Pilsen[4] neighborhood. That changed him Ma said. Took the smile off of Pa's face for the rest of his life.

I've lived around Chicago all my life. First we lived in the Pilsen neighborhood, which was one-hundred-percent "Bohunks".[5] When I was a small kid, maybe four or five, we moved across the city-line west of Chicago to Cicero. Lots of Bohunks there too. I've lived there ever since. Most people know Cicero because it was where Al Capone ran his gang. No castles in my neighborhood—just factories, railroad tracks, and a water tower. Some say the air stinks. I don't know. Except when I've been on the road, it's the only air I know. Smells normal to me. My neighborhood reminds me of a jazz cornet. I guess that's why I like the cornet more than the trumpet. The trumpet's just a little too smooth for me.

It's not been easy to be a jazzman. Jazz is a life. It's a holy ghost. That's why I wanted to write my story down. The future of jazz is with the young who have called that ghost into their hearts. Maybe hearing about what I went through to make it will help them. If I thought I could help someone who loved jazz with all their heart make it, then I'd feel good about the way my life has turned out. Some have accused me of being a soft touch and not looking out for myself, but I have always believed it is better to help than be helped; it's better to understand than be understood; it's better to give somebody a break than be given one. Isn't that right? Some of you know what I mean.

I've seen plenty in forty-two years of jazz. To live in Chicago is to live in a jazz hatchery. I saw the great New Orleans Rhythm Kings right after they came up the Mississippi River to Chicago. I saw King Oliver, Bud Freemen, Pee Wee Russel, and "Satchmo" (Louis Armstrong) when he was just starting out. And the best of them all back there in the beginning of jazz, at least for my money, was Bix Beiderbecke—a white kid out of a small Iowa river town. I called Bix a close friend. Other jazzmen have come and gone out of my life. Can't count how many of them heroin took away from me all chained up to a place I shake to think about. Others I knew were on all kinds of junk; opium and alcohol took a lot of them. I stayed clean, and I'm proud of that. A man doesn't need smack to play jazz.

Looked in the mirror the other day, or maybe it was longer than that. I can't recall, but the point is, I saw how hard my lips have become from blowing that cornet. Big round calluses. The mouthpiece of my horn fits into my lips like the male piece into the female end of a hose. I made music instead of kids. Some said I made noise. Not everybody catches the jazz bug. Those lips of mine told me how much time had passed, and how it was time to tell my story. Every song comes to an end. You can't hold a note forever.

So what goes into a life? There are things I suppose like the house and my cornet. The cornet is a Conn, and the black case got dunked in water once, so it isn't so pretty. The green felt on the inside got some mildew, and I can't get rid of the smell. Smell's worse to cover it up with some after-shave. The cornet is silver on the outside and brass inside the bell. I've shined it so much with silver cream that the name "Conn" is almost worn off. Over the years I have to admit I've grown pretty messy, but I don't play that cornet unless it's shining. Inside the case I store a bottle of valve oil to keep the valves nice and lubricated. Each of the three keys is topped off with mother of pearl. Once, during a fight in a club I was playing in, some knucklehead knocked the cornet out of my hand, and it bounced right off the edge of the stage, so there's a dent in the tube near the spit valve. Even as I'm writing this, I can feel the cornet in my hand. I can feel the dent too; it belongs there now just like the scar on my forehead I got from an angry union striker with an axe handle.

Then there's the house, but whenever I think of the house I think of the neighborhood. If I think about the neighborhood, what I'm really doing is thinking about memories. So maybe life isn't about things at all. It's about memories, the good and the bad. As much as I love it, I'm not taking my cornet with me wherever I'm going after I'm dead and buried. "Nothing crosses the Jordan with you." A Negro clarinetist told me that.

For me, smells are the strongest memories. I can remember the smells of the speakeasies,[6] and hell, they've been gone a long time. In case you're interested, the smell was sweat and booze and tobacco smoke and ladies. Still, that's not the whole soup. Something else was in it, and unless you were there, I guess you'll never understand with words. If I was playing my cornet, I'd finish this sentence with a blues note[7] instead of a period.

Lots of people kept gardens in my neighborhood when I was a kid. Now you hardly see gardens. I remember cabbages I could hardly get my arms around. I never liked the smell of the sauerkraut my Ma made from the cabbages we grew, but it tasted damn good. How are you supposed to know what a real tomato tastes like if you don't have a garden? We wasted nothing. We ate the beets fresh, pickled the extras, and ate the beet tops boiled as greens. It was beautiful to see the peas come up early in the cold wet spring soil. Ma kept a couple of chickens and a rabbit or two. I can hear them chickens cackling now. She made blood sausage—jileto in Bohemian—and I can still taste it. Sometimes she fried it with potatoes and onions.

Ma baked her own bread, and I remember that smell, especially when she made rye bread. She baked every Saturday and Sunday, even after Pa died, when she did it with a heavy bass beat. Her arms jiggled when she kneaded bread dough, but she was strong. I saw her knead with one hand and stir a bowl with the other. Her pastry crust was heavy and thick. She used lard, and it was flaky and salty. Pa didn't like it, but I didn't mind. Sometimes I want to taste that crust again with a cup of strong coffee. But it's lost somewhere now in the past.

Pa made koralka (a distilled fruit liquor) in the basement. Like almost everybody else in the neighborhood, Pa worked at the big Western Electric plant. The job kept roast pork and knedliky (dumplings) on the table. He was proud of that like he was proud of the goose he brought home every year for Christmas. Six days a week he worked at the plant. You could hear the work whistle from the house. It was louder than the church bells. I don't know how hard he worked in Bohemia, but the work he did in that plant drained him. I worked a lot of years in factories too.

    The farthest back I can remember there were still some prairies in the neighborhood. Now there's just a few empty lots filled with junk. In elementary school, a teacher said the prairies in America had once been like a great ocean with the grass moving like waves. That's a pretty thought, and I think of it sometimes—blue skies and golden and green grass—chest high—as far as you can see. When I was a boy, under the covers at night I used to pretend I was crossing the great prairies in one of them covered wagons. The thought of it put me right to sleep, the rocking back and forth, the good rich smell of the grass. Near the giant railroad yard was a small prairie I used to walk through as a shortcut. Grasshoppers jumped in front of you. We kids caught 'em, and if you squeezed their heads, something came out of their mouths that looked like tobacco juice. There were garter snakes too that wiggled in front of you, and they were as quick as Bill Evans[8] on the piano keys.

    One summer Ma and I picked onions on a farm in the middle of the prairie way west of the city in a town called Brookfield. The name sounds peaceful. Farms are peaceful. We picked onions to make some extra money from sun-up to sunset, but it was pay enough to see the color of the sun going down over the prairie—mellow as the saxophone of Coleman Hawkins[9]—swirls of purple and orange. Thunderstorms are wild over the prairie. Sometimes the dark purple clouds glow with light somebody told me is stored up lightning. Ma said Prague didn't have sunsets or thunderstorms like these.

    Ma hated digging up onions, but I loved it. I like digging, and I like the black dirt. I used to dream about those prairie farms—the hot sun, the iron-tasting well water, and the smell of that black soil. As kids we dug forts out of the soil in the prairie near the railroad yard. We made bricks of sod, and we used golden rod and cornflowers for our flags. The ground was tangled with roots. The black soil went down a few feet, and then it turned to brown clay that was as cold and damp as death. The line between the soil and clay was so straight you swore somebody did it with a ruler. I liked the black soil and hated the sticky heavy clay, but that's the way it was, both sides together, just like me I guess.

Seemed the railroad yard stretched farther away than the prairies. The flowers and grasses of the prairie grew between the rails in every place where engine oil hadn't killed them. Day and night you could hear the boxcars and tankers crashing together, being coupled and uncoupled. Back then the engines were coal-fired steam engines. I think they were beautiful, not like a woman but like a man. The sweet and sharp coal smoke from them drifted through the neighborhood and left a halo at night around the lampposts. Those engines looked strong and rough, especially at night with their big front lamps. They seemed to belong to the night. In summer, lying in bed with the window open, I heard the switch engines working the yard with their sad whistles blowing blues notes and making their shu-shu-shu sound a little like a drummer using his brushes. Funny, with all that coal smoke there was still birds singing in the morning. My teacher told me they were larks. I thank those larks because they taught me a lot about music.

Mostly the neighborhood was Bohemian, but some Dagos[10] lived there too. They had a different parish. I sneaked into the Dago parish one Sunday. Everything they were doing was the same but different. The priest mumbled in Latin, and I wondered if it was Catholic. Even their gardens were different. They grew a lot of peppers and grapes and no cabbage. My old buddy from the neighborhood, Sterek, used to say the Dagos were white niggers. Well, a lot of them became gangsters, but who could forget the trumpet of Nick LaRocca? He made the first jazz record that I know of.

Personally, I never spoke a lot of Bohemian, but I could understand. Ma and Pa fought in Bohemian, so I learned those words. They gossiped about the neighbors in Bohemian. Two newspapers that got delivered to the house were in Bohemian. Of course I knew the food words. You got smacked in school if you used the old language, so what was the point? Then after I got in jazz, nobody spoke it. None of the colored jazzmen I met who were coming up from New Orleans spoke it, that's for sure. The talk they used wasn't like anything folks in Chicago spoke. I guess you had to be born in the swamp and work in the cane fields down there to understand their talk. That's what Punch Miller[11] told me once. There was no sweeter trumpet player from those parts. He told me he came from slaves, and he even knew the plantation where his pa and grandpa worked. That has to do something to your music.

All those Negro jazzmen from New Orleans were so different to me. They had this joy and this way of talking. They made me happy being around them even when things weren't going great. Bohunks get sour, and they get dark and deep. I wonder if everyone in New Orleans is like those jazzmen. Strange, all my years in jazz, and I've never been to New Orleans or Algiers, Louisiana where I hear jazz really started. Makes me wonder what I've missed.

Some say you can't play real jazz unless you're a Negro. Well, I'll say this: jazz never would have been without them. Something in the heat down there in New Orleans mixed with the Negro, along with their sweat and toil, and out came a soup that's damn special. Still, jazz is about the heart. That's the reason an old Bohemian like me can play it. Oh, you have to have some ability. I guess there's music in my blood. I've been told I had an uncle who played in the Kaiser's band back in the old country. But jazz—you get an ear for it, and the notes keep coming in. And another thing, you don't learn to play jazz at school. You learn jazz in the gangways between apartment buildings, what rattles off the windows of nightclubs, and in a hung-over morning.

Chapter 2

How It Started

After saying you can't learn jazz in school, school is where I want to start. My school was five blocks away from the house, a couple of blocks closer than the Western Electric plant was and a couple of blocks farther away than our butcher. It looked like a factory and felt like a factory what with the bells all day. The schools in the neighborhoods around the plant even looked like the Western—same brown brick, same windows. Looked like that big factory hatched them.

Ma wrapped my school lunch in newspaper. The grease ate holes in the paper by lunchtime. Pa had a proper lunch pail, and I got one too once I left school and started at the factory. From the day I walked in the joint until the day I walked out after graduating the eighth grade, the bells always startled me—that metal clanging—no melody, no chords, no anything but hurt.

Most of the time I just grabbed my desk and held on—looking out the window when I could—watching the snow falling, rain drumming on the windows, clouds flying by. Good thing school was only mandatory through the eighth grade back then. I don't know what I would have done if it lasted longer.

Kids grew up fast, as I recall. Lots of the boys were shaving like grown men by eighth grade and the gals had tits and ass worth a careful look. There's that Dizzy Gillespie cut of *Lover Man* when the vocal part asks, "Oh lover man where can you be?" Well, I was sitting right there, third row middle seat, ready, willing, and able. Whoa, there was some juices flowing, some of it not too nice. I remember some jokers charging a penny to watch some of the girls undress in the janitor's room. Oh baby! Life ain't ever easy. That's what makes jazz a tough lover.

I don't think the school cared much. It felt like we were just passing time, like sitting on a streetcar with nothing to do but ride it to the end of the line. The principal used to call us Bohemian kids morons. Not that there weren't some morons, but the fact was they thought we were a bunch of ignorant foreigners. The Bohemian language drove a lot of teachers wild. They called it a crude language—whatever the hell that meant. They made me feel embarrassed to have parents born over there, but sometimes we got back at them by cussing them out in the old language.

One teacher was different. Her name was Miss Stepanek. Her family was from Brno. I had her for two years, seventh and eighth grade. I can't say she made me like studying. I was no genius, but some of the mopes in that class made me look like Einstein. Still, she found something good in everybody, and when other teachers weren't looking, she'd even talk in the old language. If somebody back-talked her, the rest of us took care of that guy.

I did things in school I wasn't proud of. Once, Ma was called to school 'cause I shot a pea from my shooter right in a girl's ear. So I figure it must have been in the eighth grade. I'd have to dig up my diploma, but I think it was around 1912. After I got bawled out in the principal's office in front of Ma, who was by now beet red from anger that was aimed at anyone in her path, Miss Stepanek asked if she might speak alone with Ma and me out in the hallway. When Ma got angry everybody was a target. If I could have, I would have warned Miss Stepanek. Ma held everybody responsible for making her feel insulted, embarrassed, or whatever.

I can remember it like it was yesterday. Miss Stepanek starts off by saying something like, "Thank you for taking a moment to speak with me alone."

Ma filled out a dress pretty good. She puffed up in front of Miss Stepanek, and that made her chest another half-foot bigger, and I'm telling you for true that she had the biggest tits I have ever seen on a woman. And you know what? Her tits were nothing next to the size of her forearms—real ham hocks. Well, she crossed her arms, and you couldn't even see her dress. "Whataya wannna talk about?" she says.

Miss Stepanek's voice was soft, but I had known her for a while back then, and it wasn't her normal voice. It came out of her forced and hoarse—a little Ben Webster on the saxophone if you know what I mean. "What are you thinking about for George's future?"

I swear Ma had embalming fluid in her veins. "Work," she says back.

"I'd like to see George not waste his life no matter what work he does."

"George don't waste nothin'. We don't have the money to waste. So don't tell me he's gonna be wasting."

Well, Miss Stepanek didn't back off. You got to admire her. She says calm as can be, "I don't mean, now, Mrs. Nepras. I mean ten years from now."

"Ten years, hell, who can think out ten years? I'll probably be pushing up daisies in ten years the way my stomach's been bothering me." Death was a big thing for the Bohemians in my neighborhood. They even believed no matter how bad things were, they could always get worse. No wonder I could play the Blues. Negro musicians have asked me how it is I can play the Blues. You got to be kidding me! A large sign on the front of a Bohemian restaurant in the neighborhood said in big letters, "Enjoy yourself, it's later than you think."

So Ma goes on, "I don't have time to worry about no ten years."

"I see." Miss Stepanek's face changed then. You could see she knew she wasn't going to get anywhere with Ma. Whatever else she wanted to say, she skipped. She backed off, and Ma had a satisfied grin on her face. She was used to bullying people into giving up. What she did to the green grocer, Jim Jana, made you tighten your gut like when somebody's going to take a poke at it. Miss Stepanek apologized for taking up Ma's time, then Ma showed Miss Stepanek her backside and stormed out of there.

It was maybe a week later that Miss Stepanek stops me in the hall in a way that I knew wouldn't end in a beating. She says, "What are you always humming, George?"

I says back, "I don't know, just music in my head." And I didn't know exactly what the music was, except looking back over my life, I realize now that songs stuck in my head real easy.

And then she says something like, "Maybe you should figure out how to have that music come out."

I wasn't even sure what she was driving at, but I didn't want to say I didn't know. "Maybe," I says back, figuring that answer can't get me in too much trouble.

"Ever think of playing an instrument?"

"An instrument?"

"Sure—like piano or violin. Ever thought about that?"

"No." She might as well have said, "Ever think about being a doctor?"

"What kind instruments do you like?" She says that in Bohemian.

I didn't know what to say. The sweat was already trickling down my side. For no reason at all I blurt out, "Horn."

"Any particular kind of horn?"

"Naw."

"Ok," she answers, simple as that and walks away. I didn't think anything more of it, then a week later she tells me to go to this apartment building after school. "You're going to learn how to play a trumpet." I didn't know what to think, but that day when I got home from school, Ma was in a hell of a mood, screaming and cussing and accusing me of things. She was wild in the eyes and screeching at me all out of tune. So I figure, nothing to lose by going to the apartment.

I took the streetcar, and I sat there twisting in my seat, wondering what was at the end of the ride. The address turned out to be a fancy apartment building with a walkway up the middle with three floors of apartments on each side, one apartment on each floor, and big sunrooms up front. You see a lot of them around Chicago, all brick with big, varnished wood main doors with fancy cut glass panes in them. I had never been in a building like that. The two things I remember most about stepping inside was how quiet it was and how I smelled onions frying.

I'm not sure what kept me going. I've thought a lot about that over the years. The only thing I've come up with is that I kept going because I didn't want to disappoint Miss Stepanek, even though she never said she would be disappointed if I woulda turned around and scrammed. When I walked up to the right apartment door on the top floor, I didn't hesitate and I knocked. But I'll tell you, I was as stiff from nerves as I was before my first solo.

I only found out later that the guy who opened the apartment door was one of the most famous Bohemians in America. He introduced himself without shaking hands. "I am Bohumir Kryl."[12] I don't know how Miss Stepanek knew him, but she must have. He acted like I was supposed to know who he was. I said, "Pleased to meet you." Didn't know what else to do, so he turns around and walks into the apartment, and I follow him. He didn't say nothing so I figure it was the right thing to do. I took it upon myself to close the door behind me. Outside, on the other side of the door, was what I had been, and on the inside I started to become what I am.

Kryl looked like he was in his early forties. He had this bush of hair like I've seen in pictures of lions. Some of it had gone gray, but the rest of it was the color of penny caramel candy. For a musician, he had a big chest and gave me the impression he could take care of himself. Later I found out he had been an acrobat and had worked in a circus to get to America. I noticed the shoulders of his black jacket were covered with dandruff like it had snowed on them. That only got worse over time. And finally the time came when those black frock coats got worn out and shiny, so I hear. It showed the dandruff worse, but all that happened much later. Maybe if he had cut his hair shorter the dandruff might not have been so bad, but he had his pride as a "virtuoso"—that's what he called himself. Before I met him he had been a first cornet in John Phillip Sousa's[13] band.

Well, the long and short of it was he marched me into the front room, one of the sunrooms I had seen from outside. The sun poured into the room and turned the cold day warm. The brightness made me squint. He had no drapes or blinds on the windows. I found myself staring down at the polished wood floor. I've never seen floors polished so bright. While I was doing that Kryl was fumbling with a music case. Finally he pulls a cornet out and inspects it with squinting eyes. The horn shone a deep copper color, and the sunlight danced off of it like it was playing music by itself. "This horn," he said he had used "playing in the Kaiser's band back in Europe." The valves weren't set the way I knew cornets oughta be. These came out in an angle instead of being arranged on top of the horn.

He starts to play, and the notes bounce around and jump into my head, perfect notes, crystal notes that send every nerve in my head singing. Those notes blew up and shrank inside my head like somebody had a bellows at my ear, pumping air into my head, sparking a flame that danced inside me. I wanted to hold my ears not because it hurt but because I wasn't sure how much I could take. Even when he stopped, I kept hearing the notes like the sound of a church bell after somebody stops ringing it.

Then he kind of licks his lips and starts in again but this time he triple-tongues. At the time, I didn't know what you called it, I only knew it was like three different cornets playing, no, three cornets talking together. I remember standing there in that sunroom with my hands jammed in my pockets, squinting in the bright light, not knowing what to do but feeling like my mind was outside my body, and I was watching all this from somewhere, I don't know, from the ceiling maybe.

After he stops the second time, he just stares at me like he was expecting me to say something. What could I say? This wasn't like nothing at school, and it sure as hell wasn't like home. Those dark eyes of his made me feel uncomfortable. His music came out of his horn, not his eyes. What did he want? Finally, he says, "You think you can make the notes come out of here?" He points to the bell of his cornet that just then caught the sun, and light came off it like a lick of flame. He doesn't wait for my answer. Instead, he hands me the cornet and says, "Try it," but this time in Bohemian.

So I answer, "Pokusim se" (I'll try). I take a deep breath and let loose into the horn. The vibration rattles my front teeth, and the sound was louder than the train whistles in the railway yard. Kryl put his hands to his ears, but he didn't smile or frown. "So there, so you can make a sound. That's the beginning." From then on we worked together. He showed me how to hold my lips and how the sound changed depending on the angle you blew into the mouthpiece. He counted and kept saying, "Bop, bop, bop, bop," and I was to make a sound every time he said it. He told me those were quarter-notes.

Never in my life did an hour go faster. When he said the hour was over, I thought it was a joke. Then I realized it was time to settle up. "How much?" I asked. He seemed insulted.

"I don't deal with money," he says kind of snooty.

"But who do I gotta pay?" I says back.

"It's taken care of. Don't bother me again about money. Just be here again next week."

I came back the next week, and the next one, and the week after that. I was no jazzman yet. Kryl taught the classics and marches. I'm not sure jazz had even been invented when I first walked into Kryl's apartment. It was still stewing in the pot down in New Orleans. Still, the doors were slamming shut and opening, and jazz and me were coming closer and closer to meeting every day that passed.

I learned that Thursdays were the days Kryl taught students, some in horn but also piano and violin. One day he was running late, so I was cooling my heels in his living room. In the sunroom I heard a violin. I could hear Kryl's voice too and then I heard a girl's voice answering him. That got my curiosity up. Finally, they come out of the room, and I see this young lady with dark curly hair parted down the middle and a fine dress with two roses pinned to her waist. No young women wore dresses like that in my neighborhood. It was so delicate, and I remember it to this day. It was cream-colored with brown stitching running down from her shoulders to her waist in a design maybe of flowers. The same stitching was on the wrists of the dress too. The dress rustled when she moved, trapping my attention like a catchy piano tune you hear coming from somewhere when you're out on the street.

Kryl helped her on with a coat. That's when we saw each other, and she smiled and said hello. Kryl says, "Master Nepras, let me introduce you to Miss Stella Vraz." Never in my life have I ever seen a young lady's eyes twinkle like Stella's. She had pretty teeth and pretty hands and a long smooth neck. I stood up of course. I learned a couple of the right moves in the neighborhood. We weren't animals.

That night I had grown-up thoughts. I don't mean sex. That was nothing new. What I thought about was how complicated life was, how Ma and Pa had come from Bohemia and how we had moved from Pilsen near 18th Street to Cicero, and how I get Miss Stepanek for a teacher, and then I'm all of a sudden learning music from a master, and then this beautiful young woman stands right in front of me and smiles. And then bam, it comes to you how you can't control nothing, so I guess you just let it happen.

Chapter 3

Funerals and More Funerals

Don't know what it's like in the real Bohemia, but in "Little Bohemia" in Chicago death was a big thing. That sign on the restaurant I already mentioned, "Enjoy Yourself, It's Later Than You Think", didn't really have much to do with enjoying anything. It was a reminder like your tax is due. But nobody needed reminding. The priest mostly talked about death at Mass. Communion was about the LAST supper, and after Mass, people stood around and gossiped about death and dying.

"Jendrasek keeled over getting out of the bathtub."

"Ben Blaha's liver was the size of a watermelon."

"Forty-three she was, and she never saw it coming."

"Jesus, Mary and Holy St. Joseph, I didn't even recognize him at the end. They had to close the casket!"

I went to more funerals and wakes by the time I was ten than baseball games, weddings, and christenings all put together. I could name more dead people than living ones. So it shouldn't surprise nobody that us Bohunks made a huge production out of funerals. We even had our own cemetery, "The Bohemian National Cemetery"[14] up on the north side near Pulaski and Foster Avenues. The joint was practically stampeded on to buy plots. Some of these old Bohunks didn't own a pot to piss in, pardon my French, but they owned a plot at Bohemian National. It was something to brag about, like owning box seats at Comiskey Park.[15]

In a special strange way, funerals were the one thing my neighborhood had in common with the Negroes of New Orleans. Brass bands played at funerals, and the musicians wore military style uniforms, and I understand that's just the way it is in New Orleans. They played sad music until after the dead person was potted, then, at the dinner that followed, they played happy stuff. The big difference is that at the Bohemian funerals, the sad stuff was mostly out of the classics, and the happy music was polkas. In New Orleans, it's spirituals and then jazz. I wish I could get on the telephone and dial somebody up in Prague and ask if people in the real Bohemia have the same custom as their cousins in Chicago. Of course since Communism and the Iron Curtain you just can't pick up a telephone and dial somebody over there. For all you'd know you might start an atomic war. For us Bohemians in Chicago, the Iron Curtain is a sad thing. It's like the country we came from disappeared off the earth and erased our history.

The polka music was supposed to lift your spirits, but it's come to mean the blues to me. I remember one funeral. Maybe it was even Pa's. I can still hear that polka band playing. Uncle Jaromir sat across from me. His chin was shiny with duck grease. He looks at me and says, "Chutna" (tasty). He goes on, "First rate Muscovy Duck!" A satisfied smile was plastered all over his face, making him look like he thought he had cheated death and was gonna live forever. Hope he enjoyed it. He died six months later.

In tough times I've had to play polka music at plenty of funerals to make a dime. Being a jazzman is a hard life. It's hard for me to stand up on the stage and keep smiling. Out in front of me the polka dancers are having fun, twirling around, but not me. I come home after that, and I almost don't have the energy to climb the front stairs. I think of all those coffins belonging to people I cared about and of Uncle Jaromir and that stupid grin with the grease smeared on his chin. Then I lay in bed, and the polka music keeps playing over and over, and I keep falling deeper and deeper into sadness. The blues don't leave me for days.

A memory comes to me. Ma, Pa, and me had gone to a funeral. It was dark out, the way it gets in December when the days are short and the clouds block out the stars. We sat around the table eating sandwiches 'cause we had our big meal at the banquet after the funeral. I can hear Pa saying to me, "Hey, put some meat on that sandwich. You wanna grow up to be a runt?" Meat was important to Pa. Being able to have meat on the table meant he had made it.

Pa sent me to the bar around the corner to get his beer pail filled. Chicago has always had a lot of bars, but before Prohibition, my God they were everywhere, especially in the Bohemian neighborhood. Bohemians like their beer. Back then there was nothing wrong with a kid going to get his old man's beer pail filled. The foam popped up through the lid. I liked to take a whiff of it up close. Smelled like steel. The bartender put the refill on Pa's tab. Neighborhood bars have a sweet and doughy smell I've always liked—sweet from cheap bourbon and doughy from the beer. I like the darkness too like a confessional on Friday night. Somebody drinking at the bar with his foot up on the brass rail, beads of sweat dripping down his cold schooner would call out, "Hey kid, tell your old man hello." It made me feel important. Sometimes if the guy was good and soused he'd flip me a nickel. Then I'd hear the guy tap the shot glass next to his schooner. It meant he wanted another shot. That's mostly what the men drank in the neighborhood—a beer and a shot.

Anyway, when I get home, I can tell something ain't right, but nobody says nothing. Pa pours himself a glass of beer and a small one for me. It was normal for a kid to have a small glass of beer with his old man. To a Bohemian beer is just liquid bread. Well after a few glasses of beer Pa seems to have gotten over whatever was bothering him. Ma's reading the newspaper. But then as regular as the lunch whistle at the Western, Ma did her usual and said something to insult Pa and—Bam!—It was Saturday night at the fights.[16]

Pa had black curly hair, and that's not so typical in Bohemians. Ma knew that. Something made Ma turn mean all of a sudden. Out of nowhere, she'd turn red like a beet and sneer, "With that nose of yours and that hair, you must be a zid (Jew)."

"If I'm a zid, why did you marry me?"

"I was drunk."

"Ha!"

"And if you ain't a zid you're a cikan (gypsy)."

With that Pa started tearing his hair and howling. I swear Ma grinned every time she got Pa so worked up. Well, Pa sees her grinning and so from the corner of the kitchen he grabs a piece of 2x4 he was going to use to swap out a rotten piece in the chicken coop. Pa cracked that piece of wood so hard over the table, it stung my ears. That quieted Ma down. She damn well knew if she pushed any more Pa's next move was to use it on her head.

Just when things quieted down, Ma took a chance and mumbled, "ZCBJ", and pretended to spit. Pa was playing solitaire and sipping beer and didn't notice or hear, thank God, because if he had, he would have killed her. See Ma was Catholic, and Catholics in the neighborhood hated the ZCBJ[17]. She always crossed herself and said, "The ZCBJ works for the devil."

That night laying in bed I admit I couldn't figure things out. What was the sense of making life miserable? We had just been to a funeral. Life for that person was over. Death was coming for all of us. Didn't it make sense to enjoy life when you can? Why rip each other apart? In those times I'd pray for God to put me at rest, and He did. Somehow, in those times alone after a funeral and a couple of hours of screaming, I always got the message that I was supposed to play music. I'm not saying God came to me and said, "George, play music!" It was more that I knew, knew for certain, that music was what I was supposed to do. And the next day when I woke up that thought was alive in my belly, and the funeral and fight of the day before was forgotten. In bed I listened to the rhythm of the early morning, Pa snoring in the room next to me, and Ma kneading bread in the kitchen. It was going to be all right.

Chapter 4

More About My Life as a Kid— My First Job

Every couple of weeks or so because Pa always said, "Ma can't bake kolaczky[18] worth a shit," we went to Jana's Bakery. There's no bakery in the world better, and I still go there. That's why I have a spare tire around my middle. Sometimes when I wear an undershirt in the summer, I don't go out because it embarrasses me to have that tire jiggling around. I do ten, even twenty sit-ups, but it doesn't go away. When I first earned a few bucks, I'd go by Jana's and maybe get a few dulky. Dulky are like doughnuts filled with prune or apricot and then covered with unsweetened whipped cream. I'd eat them and finish off a quart of milk. Anyway, that's mostly about me later. I want to tell you first about how I grew up.

In the fall, Jana's makes a grape kolac[19] that'll bring tears to your eyes it's so good. In June are the strawberry desserts. On a Saturday the old Bohunks are lined up at the door before it opens at 6:30. The display window is filled with everything you could imagine. There's Kolac out of nuts, butterscotch, and fruit, houska[20], poppy seed cake, potato flour bread, salty horn rolls with a sausage baked inside, and big babovka[21].

Then there was the butcher shop, but butcher shops aren't the same anymore. Then, the white tiled floor was spread with sawdust. In the back they made their own sausage. There were ducks, chickens, and bazant (pheasant) hanging behind the counter with their beautiful tan feathers still on them. Back then we ate a lot of sweet breads and liver. Ma soaked the liver in milk to take the bitterness out, and she only made calves liver. God, it was delicious. Next to the counter was a big wooden barrel filled with garlic dill pickles. Each pickle was five or six inches long. The shop was alive with the Bohemian language. People seemed happy there and weren't worrying it was later than you think. All the chatter in the butcher shop reminded me of a tinkling piano, maybe like Bud Powell.[22]

    I watched Pa shave through a crack in the bathroom door. Pa didn't like to be disturbed when he shaved. He stropped his razor to quarter-beat time. Pa shaved with his undershirt on. I do the same now. Some things get grooved into your life early and never change. Some things you wish could change; some things you don't want to change. That's part of why I like Jana's bakery so much. It's been the same all these years. I learned early to accept what was, be grateful for the good that comes along. That's a Christian way to be, but if I'm honest, I have to say I got that way so I could get by. The other choice was something so dark I can't describe it. I can only feel it, but I promise you, I've looked down into the pit, into that nighttime with no bottom. It's much easier to be happy about life after looking down there.

    For my first job, I sold newspapers out in front of the Western Electric. Maybe I was ten. I stood out there in front of the Western's main gate. My memory has it only in winter, but that can't be right. I wore Pa's old overcoat, and it dragged on the ground until I figured out how to pin it up. I was there before the sun was up, and I stayed until just a few minutes before school. I watched the sun break its cherry every morning like it was the first time and spill all over the sky. The color framed the smoke stacks. Chicago is a cold place in the winter before the sun comes up. If it was a good morning for making money, I bought a coffee and a piece of buttered bread from the buffet wagon parked nearby.

    Every morning the newspaper wagon came. The guy on the wagon and my boss was Gus O'Dowd. He was an old man who never did me wrong. If I made a mistake, he made it right. I used to tease him, "Hey Gus, what is O'Dowd? That a Polish name?"

    He'd laugh every time. Gus sucked on an old cigar and kept a pencil jammed behind his ear. He'd say something like, "How many papers you got left kid?"

    Maybe I'd say back, "Forty."

    "Forty? Don't nobody read?" Gus was a joker too.

    "Guess not Gus." And I'd load them on the wagon.

While Gus did his arithmetic, I talked to the sorrel named Shine that pulled the wagon. I always kept something for her, a piece of carrot or apple I had sneaked out of the kitchen. She let me hold her around the neck and cuddle up close. The sweet leather smell of her bridle is still in my nose. Her breaths came in big warm gushes down the inside of my collar. I rubbed her nose between her blinders, and she stayed steady. Came to learn over the years that every change brings something new, but also takes something away. No diesel truck could ever replace Shine. Don't think for a minute Shine don't still live in my music.

The main gate of the Western was a great place to peddle newspapers. The guards all knew me, and they waved to me when they opened the gate with a rattling of metal bar and chain. The guards were proud of their keys and brass buttons. Beside the English papers I sold *Svornost*, *Spravedlnost*, and *Denni Hlasatel*.[23] Pa read *Svornost*.[24] Bohemians like to read, and I sold a lot of papers, so I was an earner. As fast as I could hand them out, they bought them. They were impatient and always grousing, "Hey kid, hurry up," but I don't remember anybody cheating me.

One minute it was quiet outside the gate. The plant stood sleeping with lazy steam and smoke leaking out its chimneys. In the cold mornings the wind took the smoke and feathered it high up in the air. Then in the next minute, the workers started coming down the wide sidewalk, crossing the street, emptying out of streetcars. Up close they looked tired and smelled of coffee, tobacco, and last night's beer. Way off in the distance as they all came together at the main gate and melted into one big bobbing river of men. They headed to the plant down the even wider company street. From way off, they all seemed to turn gray.

Don't know when these men read their papers. There was no time on the production line unless you wanted to get fired. Pa read his newspaper in the evening while Ma heated water for his bath. Pa always got meat at dinner; I didn't. Still, I never went hungry. Usually we drank coffee at dinner. Only later when I got older did it bother my sleep and stomach.

Pa was so careful the way he folded his newspaper. He was a perfectionist. Maybe not in other things, but in music I'm a perfectionist, too. A lot of people think jazz has no rules, no discipline. Jazz is discipline. A jazz song might sound like all the pieces have fallen apart, but in truth, all the pieces fit together.

Pa was competitive too. You should have seen him at the factory picnics. Those picnics were wonderful—an accordion here, a violin there, a little child's voice and the smell of stale beer and *grilovana klobasa* (grilled sausage) in the air. Pa didn't allow me to talk to him when he was playing horseshoes. In fact, he didn't want nobody talking to him. Still, I know he liked me to watch. Even when he threw a ringer, his expression never changed. That's how much he concentrated.

If I close my eyes, I can see and hear those horseshoe games again. *Ping* when the shoes hit the metal stakes. *Thud* when they landed in the sand, or *clank* when one shoe hit another one. Arguments went on nonstop in Bohemian and English. Pa held his own. He didn't like to lose. Sometimes I walked off and lay down in the tall grass to watch the clouds pass. I've always loved summer most of all.

Personally, I was never too good in sports. I never joined the Sokol.[25] God gave me talent in music. We've got to be grateful for what we've got. I tell the kids in the neighborhood that every chance I can get, but they laugh and call me "old man." I did all right in baseball. Sometimes our parish, St. Adelbert[26], played the Dagos from their parish. They had to stop those games by order of the Archdiocese because of the brawls.

Pa watched me play once. I was batting, and there was a close call at first base. I knew I was out. Everybody started pitching a fit, but I said, "Hey, I was out fair and square." I told the team, "We'll get them next inning."

Pa said to me later, "Don't admit nothing. That's why there's an umpire. You shut up. Got it?"

I didn't always make outs. I got my share of hits. Once I remember getting a triple that won the game. Had to slide into third. The problem was I was playing in my Sunday shoes, and I caught hell when I got home. Ma boxed my ears good. Ma and Pa called me a "silly goose." Now it makes me laugh.

CHAPTER 5

Learning About Syncopation and Other Music Lessons

Sometimes I hung out in a produce market after school that was a couple of miles from the house. Some of the vendors gave me odd jobs if they saw me standing around with my hands jammed in my pockets. I made a couple of quarters loading crates of fruit onto wagons or stacking empty crates out back of the vendors' stalls. That market is where I learned syncopation though I didn't know it at the time, and it was a couple of years before Kryl ever gave me a music lesson.

In that market everything is offbeat. Wagons are parked every which way. The traffic goes everywhere and nowhere. The horses are jittery with their nostrils wide open and their hoofs beating a tattoo on the cobblestones. Men stand up and shout from their wagons numbers that make no sense unless you're in on the deal. Motor trucks creep along, too. In the winter you can see waves of heat coming off the engines. Their horns sound like trumpets with mutes jammed in them.

Teamsters stand around oil drums filled with burning busted up vegetable and fruit boxes, drinking steaming coffee and talking about getting laid. They stick their hands over the flame like our priest does over the cup. The wood boxes they bust up have these colorful, pretty pictures pasted to their sides of fruit orchards, vineyards, tomatoes with eyes and smiling faces wearing a royal crown, and sunsets over plowed California fields. Each furrow disappears into a point that vanishes way far away. In the snow and ice of winter are smashed tomatoes and oranges. But the snow isn't exactly snow five days after a storm. It's a dirty stew. Everything's running late and a half-beat out of step. The men's voices are flat and the crates scraping as they come off the wagons sound sharp.

Something about me was different. The wind rattled the door at night and put me to sleep. To me, the moon seemed brighter than the sun. I felt alone on a busy street. I liked the nighttime best just before dawn. During an August dry spell I noticed how good the grass grew under where Ma hung the clothes to dry. A dirty market, a smokestack, Jana's Bakery, the cornflowers that grew along the wall of the Western Electric—it all stayed inside my head like pictures in a wallet. I had to wrap up this difference I had real tight. Mostly, nobody knew how offbeat I was. My foreman at the factory said of me, "George does his job. He does what he's told." I'm proud of that because it meant my offbeat side wasn't leaking out. It took a lot of energy to keep it locked away. A man's got to keep roast pork and knedliky on the table. Being offbeat is a good way to lose your day job.

Sometimes I imagined myself like the lunches Ma wrapped up tight in newspaper. Everything was okay for a while, but by eleven or so the grease began to leak through. Big spots of grease kept getting bigger and bigger. Finally the paper started to break up. That lunch was busting out by noon. That wrapped up lunch was me. I could only keep myself bottled up so long. I practically had to tape my mouth shut to keep the music from coming out. If you looked hard enough I imagine you could see the notes leaking out my ears—sixteenths and quarter-notes and eighths. Everything bouncing out of me offbeat—Dixieland style all syncopated.

I remember one late spring in front of Kryl's apartment building, lilacs bloomed. It was one of those first days after a long Chicago winter and wet cold spring where I felt comfortable being outside wearing nothing on top but a shirt. On my way to Kryl's, the windows on the streetcar had been open, and the breeze that blew through the car was a waltz. From down on the pavement, with the smell of the sweet lilacs and the bright new green everywhere, I heard string music falling like a shower from the open windows of Kryl's sunroom. I recognized Stella's violin, and I heard a viola and a cello, too.

Stella had been practicing in a quartet for a while. My lesson always followed hers, so we usually had ten minutes or so to chat at the end of her lesson and before mine began, so that's how I knew about the quartet. When I asked her what they were practicing, she'd act all coy and say she couldn't say because she was too shy. Well, even then I knew it was a kind of game we were playing. And I knew she really liked me pestering her about her music. Even though I knew it was a game, my heart stopped to see her lovely face blush and her eyes turn down with her long eyelashes covering those sparkling eyes like a fan. Above everything else, the thing I remember most about her at that time was how when she turned her head away, I saw the long muscle of her neck stretch from her ear to the top of her high collar. A tiny earring dangled over the line of that muscle. It was all so beautiful it hurt.

"Give me a hint, Stella."

"I can't, George."

"Not even if I give you the prettiest apple in the store?"

She had a way of laughing with the tip of her tongue between her teeth. She did that then. "Maybe."

Kryl came out of his room. "So Master Nepras, are your lips sufficiently warmed up?"

Stella did blush for real then. I jumped up. Kryl didn't waste a minute of a lesson. The cornet and trumpet were his special instruments. He was hard on me because of that, but it wasn't a bad kind of hard.

During my lesson, Kryl sat behind a table that might have been in somebody's dining room. Nothing was kept on top of it. It was a light wood, and you could see the grain waving through the length of it. Kryl rested his elbows on the table and folded his hands to prop up his chin. His eyes and mouth were serious and that made him seem angry. From there he watched everything—my posture, my breathing, and my timing. Over and over he had me practice bar after bar, exercise after exercise, scale after scale. I knew my notes spilled out the sunroom windows and splashed below. I wanted them to be perfect notes in case Stella was listening from below. Instead of getting tired I grew stronger from the drills. My energy seemed forever. Trying to add up the hours I practiced would be like counting the drops in an April shower.

Mostly Kryl wanted to teach me the classics. He had a special affection for modern French composers like Ravel. Kryl said he had known the great Bohemian composer, Antonin Dvorak.[27] It seemed Kryl could play anything. I learned what Bach sounded like from Kryl's demonstrations. Sometimes we worked on march music too, and Kryl sometimes told me of his association with Sousa and his audition with him. These stories were like dreams to me, and at home in bed, I had auditions with great bandleaders too.

It was through the classics that I recall maybe one of my sweetest memories of Stella. On the way out of a lesson one day, she pressed into my hand a ticket to a concert her quartet was to perform at the Sokol hall. The ticket she passed me was warm and moist. She must have been secretly holding it in her hand for a while. I held it all the tighter. She didn't say even one word, but then music speaks without words.

Time passed slowly while I waited for that Saturday evening. Stella wore a fancy formal dress, and she looked like a woman instead of a girl, and that made me feel like a boy. I wished I was five years older. I wore my best, what Ma had me put on to go to Mass, a corduroy jacket and a ribbon tie. The jacket was too small and too heavy for the warm night.

Kryl himself introduced the concert. I can remember as if it was today. He said something like, "Ladies and gentlemen, tonight you will hear the music of the contemporary and renown French composer, Claude Debussy. This wonderful quartet of young musicians will perform the *String Quartet in G minor*. For the second part of the program you will be treated to yet another example of modern genius and from yet another Frenchman, Maurice Ravel's *String Quartet in F*. These young musicians seated behind me have exceeded my expectations in every way."

That meant Stella exceeded his expectations. I was so proud. From the darkened audience I could not help but stare at her as she sat in her seat, her back so straight, her beautiful violin held so straight. Light glistened off of it and off her hair. They were of a similar color. I wanted to shout, "That's my Stella." If she really was mine, oh, if she could be? After that night, Stella became the rhythm behind every song I played. When you're young—and I was probably only seventeen—you know everything's going to work out fine.

Those quartets that evening taught me about how wonderful music could be. To be honest, I can't remember the music in detail anymore. It was so long ago, and I haven't been around music like that for a very long time, except for one concert, and I'll tell you about that later. All that's left are impressions like someone took a brush and painted long pale streaks of color on a wall. But I remember the power of it too, the way it spun me around—sad, happy, on edge, floating, daydreaming, concentrating. Of course there's no denying, it's hard to know how much was the music and how much was the pleasure of watching

Stella. Years later there was that song that's become a jazz standard, *Stella by Starlight*.[28] It goes in one verse:

> "That's Stella by Starlight
> And not a dream
> My heart and I agree
> She's everything on this earth to me."

Well when I heard *Stella by Starlight* the first time, seeing her at that concert came to me and has always come to me since, every time I hear it or play that song, and I mean to tell you, I play it every chance I get.

So after the concert, I went down to congratulate Stella. She was beaming, all rosy cheeks and the most wonderful smile. Stella had green and brown eyes that were set deep and teased you every time their light fell on you. I saw Stella's eyes flash away, then I was aware that someone was standing next to me.

"Papa," Stella said, "This is a friend of mine from Doctor Kryl's school."

I got to tell you I gulped. And he says to me something like, "Well young man, I'm pleased to meet you," and then, "What's your name?"

I croaked something out all dry-mouthed. He says, "Oh, Nepras, so you're a Bohemian boy then?" He asked me what instrument I played, and Stella jumped in right on the upbeat, "Oh Papa, he's the most marvelous trumpet player."

"That's Bohumir Kryl's instrument." Then he says, and I could have dropped on the floor, "George, why don't you join us for pastry and coffee to celebrate Stella's concert?"

After that, I'm not sure what I said 'cause I was floating. We went to this fancy place with shiny wood walls and electric lights. And the place had a telephone. That telephone kept ringing, and I just had to watch the guy put the receiver to his ear. What a gadget! Of course nobody pays it much attention now, but I still don't understand how it works. We didn't have no telephone at home until only a few years ago or maybe fifteen.

I didn't know what to order. Nothing looked like the buchtas Ma baked. Finally, Mr. Vraz had pity on me and says, "May I make a suggestion, George?"

"Yes sir," was my reply. Out comes this chocolate cake that was soft, a little bit of Chet Baker[29] on trumpet. Whew, it was good, and the coffee had whipped cream on it. I'd never seen that before.

Mr. and Mrs. Vraz called it "Schlagobers". What the hell? Turned out Schlagobers was Austrian-German for whipped cream, Mr. Vraz said. Mr. Vraz had worked in the Kaiser's government and had lived with Mrs. Vraz in Vienna[30] for a while before they had come to Chicago. He had family living in Prague, Vienna, and Chicago. From letters and talking to them, he decided Chicago was the place to be to get a fresh start on things. That's pretty much why most of the Bohunks came over. Well, Mr. Vraz worked at the Western, but not on the line like most of the immigrants. He was an engineer, which meant he was smart, and sat in an office figuring things out and being a decision maker. But he wasn't stuck up. As he said, "The Bohemians have to stick together over here, don't they George?" I guess he meant it because I learned later he devoted a lot of his spare time to helping with the Czech Benevolent Society.[31]

I had the common sense to look at Mr. Vraz when he was talking to me, and I answered him and Mrs. Vraz the best I could, but for the rest of the time I watched Stella. Stella ate her cake like her mother with her little finger sticking out when she held her fork. If Ma did that it woulda looked like a big dill pickle sticking out there. Stella's finger was lovely and long and slender. I could see why she played the violin.

After that I was invited with the Vraz family a lot, enough to make Ma jealous. She called me "stuck up," and said I "looked down my nose at the people in the neighborhood." Pa said he "Didn't give a shit," about me spending time with the Vraz family as long as I didn't join in on "The Western's exploiting management shit." Neither had much good to say about me playing music. I can tell you one thing, my cornet playing was getting better and better. Kryl said, "Nepras, you have potential young man." So I did what I'd been practicing for years, I put Ma and Pa out of my mind as best I could. It was music and Stella, Stella and music. Life was a dream *Way down yonder in New Orleans.*[32]

I remember the dining room table the way Mrs. Vraz set it. The cloth napkins had lace edges and in the middle was embroidered a V for Vraz. Mrs. Vraz told me that they had brought these napkins all the way from Prague and told me about how wonderfully the lace in Prague was made. When she talked about Prague there was a little sadness in her voice, just a touch, and I wondered if she wished she was back there. But I never asked Stella about it.

My playing became "sharp and dedicated", whatever that means. It was what Kryl said. He even smiled once when I surprised him at how fast I learned a hard piece. Sometimes Stella and I played together. That was sweet. Her parents enjoyed that. They'd sit in their front parlor holding hands and listening to the two of us play. Everything, and I mean everything that worried or upset me about life, disappeared at those times.

I will tell you now one of the most special memories of my life. It had nothing to do with my career in jazz, or maybe it had everything to do with my jazz. One evening after Stella and I played, I was getting ready to leave. She still held her violin and bow. She wore a starched crumply long dress. We were standing in the vestibule of the Vraz house. Mr. and Mrs. Vraz were facing us, and we were kind of jammed in the doorway. I don't recall exactly what we were saying, but I took my right arm and put it on the small of Stella's pretty back. I knew her parents couldn't see what I had done. Ever so gradually I felt Stella give way to my touch, ever so little, come closer until I could faintly feel the top of her thigh through the material of her dress and my trouser leg. When she did this, when she came closer, even with all the loud gay talking, I heard that dress rustle.

Chapter 6

Life Turns Upside Down

Sometimes in Chicago in the summer when there is going to be a great big storm with lightning and maybe hail and even a twister, the clouds that roll low over the neighborhood glow. I've seen them glow orange, and I've seen them glow green. For a while it's quiet and then you hear the drumbeat of thunder like tom toms in the Benny Goodman band way off. That was 1914 for me.

If you lived in the Bohemian neighborhoods of Chicago, 1914 was a big shock. All of a sudden there was a war because some Serb plugged the Arch-Duke of the Austro-Hungarian Empire.[33] Next thing you know Germany, France, Russia, Italy, and England are in on the deal. Figures the dagos would fight the Austrians. Well, the Germans and the Austrians were looked at mostly as the bad guys. We Bohemians couldn't go around helping the people in the Old Country. We had to keep feelings to ourselves. There was some who were carrying on about a chance for a free Bohemia. What could I do about it being something like sixteen and wet behind my ears?

"There's families to worry about back there," some said, but this was 1914, mostly people had long cut themselves off from back there. More than a month it took for a letter to arrive from some second cousin, Karel Halak, to send money and to report so and so died. Ma shrugged her shoulders. Pa told me to "mind my own business" when I asked if we was going to do something. He never said nothing else about the war I can remember except, "War's what you get from Kings and capitalists." That he said all the time.

I mean we were here, and they were there. Nobody was going back. If you was really lonely for there, all you could do was get over it. The jobs were here, and the killing was there. And money? Who had money to send anywhere? We were all trying to get by. Nobody was getting rich working on some factory line.

I guess they thought back there everybody was rich in America, and the streets were made outta gold. So 1914 was like the glowing clouds, and bad as it was, it was still only the thunder in the distance.

The real storm for the Bohemians in Chicago broke out on July 24, 1915. That was the day of the big Western Electric picnic. Ma, Pa, and I were supposed to go, but Ma got into some argument with somebody who was organizing buses or wagons to get to the pier where the steamboats were leaving from to go over to the Indiana dunes on Lake Michigan.

So Ma says, "I ain't going nowhere that blazen (fool) organizes."

Pa said, "I could give a shit, just shut up about it already."

So we didn't go. Stella asked if I wanted to go with her family. I thought I better stay at home the way my Ma was feeling. I made some excuse or other. Stella was hurt. You could see it in her face, and that hurt face is with me still. Her pretty pink lips all turned down. It's there burned into me. I should have been with her. No matter how many times I go to Confession about it, I never felt the sin was forgiven. The only way I can forget it is to die.

The neighborhood was a ghost town what with everybody on the excursion. We were just sitting down to lunch when word started to trickle back. We saw some neighborhood people walking down the street. They shouldn't have come back for five or six hours yet.

Pa opened the door and shouted out, "Hey, what the hell are you doing back so soon?"

Ma was at the front room window peeking around the lace curtain the way she always did, and I was peeking from behind Pa's shoulder. I remember like it was yesterday. The people were walking like they were waist deep in roast pork gravy. They slowly turned to Pa, "Didn't you hear?"

"Hear what, for Christ's sake?"

"The Eastland[34] went down."

"What the hell's the Eastland?" But I knew and so did Ma. We had seen the fliers. It was the big excursion boat that was taking a lot of the people to the picnic.

"It's a ship, Nepras, and it sank, and everybody's drowned."

"Holy shit," Pa answered, and Ma crossed herself. For me, it was like I got dropped from the roof, a long fall with your stomach floating, and then a crash. I remember walking up to my room. I knew. I didn't need nobody to tell me, so I just stayed in my room. I waited. I guess I waited for the news. My mind played a couple of staccato notes of hope. Maybe Stella didn't die. I kept thinking of her sitting at the concert with her violin on her lap. I loved her, you know. I don't know if I had said that, but it's true, maybe the truest thing in my life to that point.

Looking back, I know I was a child. I've learned what a complicated thing love is—especially the way your own self has to be the background music, even the back-beat, but never since have I been sent flying like I was with Stella. No one ever had to explain a Gershwin love song to me after Stella.

Ma didn't know what to make of me. Every piece of my body felt like bags of sand. At one point, I swear I felt Stella's spirit next to me. I didn't even have the strength to blow my horn. Two days later I heard for sure; the whole Vraz family had died. I never went to Kryl's for a trumpet lesson after that. Kryl never wrote me or called on me. And Ma and Pa, they didn't care. Music got pushed out of my life out of sadness—because I didn't know what to do with my sadness, so I destroyed whatever reminded me of Stella and whatever gave me joy. I never went to the funeral Mass. Twenty-nine in our parish died. In fact I didn't go to Mass for a long time after. All that was life was now death.

For a long time in bed at night I relived what must have been Stella's last minutes. I've never been able to swim. Nobody ever taught me, and there weren't any pools in my neighborhood except the pools of water in the potholes. It wasn't easy to get to Lake Michigan for me. But that doesn't mean I couldn't imagine what it was like to drown. All the papers had pictures of the Eastland, so I know what that boat looked like. Had Stella been on top or on a floor below when the ship turned over? Was her Papa and Ma there to hold her, or did they get split up? Was it black? It must have been. Oh Stella, how scary it must have been—that cold water, the dark, and the water pushing you. Did you try to scream? I would have. Was it then the water rushed in your mouth? I'm sure you were wearing one of your pretty dresses. Did it float around you? Oh Stella, you didn't deserve that? You were so pretty. Sometimes I woke up gasping for air and sweating all over. I imagined drowning. In my sleep I must have stopped breathing.

For some people, life is like a spring that gently unwinds. They get older, and you slowly see the changes. Like knowing the look of a good horse at the track, you can bet pretty sure when that coil's going to finally unwind in those folks. Old man Kalucek was like that. Finally, he looked like an old log. Others though, others like Stella, they burn bright, and then they're gone.

For a long time after, the only pleasure in my life seemed to come from pretending about me and Stella. It was the place I could go to smile and be happy. Life got back to normal for Ma and Pa. The screaming at each other hardly missed a beat. The Western whistle never missed blowing once. Everybody just swallowed the shock and marched back to work except for me. How do you crawl out of a pit that's so deep? And I was a kid. I realize that now, but it doesn't mean hurt couldn't replace the tune I'd been whistling in my head. All I had left were the little scenes my imagination made, holding Stella tight under the covers with a blizzard outside, going someplace with Stella on the train, playing music together, and her cooking nice things and using those napkins her Ma brought from Prague. To this day I wonder whether that pain made me a jazzman or damaged my music somehow forever.

Uncle Tomas pushed me into a job at The Western I didn't want. There's a lot more to tell about that, but I'll save that for later. The main thing to understand is that The Western job filled up hours that disappeared, and I have no idea where the hours went. They're some place written down like Gus's bookkeeping, but who knows where, maybe with the angels.

The bad things didn't stop. The next thing I was aware of it was 1918, and the country was going to war to fight the "Huns."[35] It wasn't good to have a German name. Kryl ran off to lead an Army band so I heard, but I had no desire to see him off. Somehow or another the Bohemians around the neighborhood believed the war would end with Bohemia being free of the Austrians, but I couldn't quite figure that one out. The parades didn't matter to me, and the rallies at the Sokol Hall for an independent Czech country was something for other people.

One thing I'll tell you, everybody was for America to win the war. The Huns sunk the passenger ship Lusitania[36] for God Almighty, and it was filled with innocent women and children just like the Eastland. That was low on the part of the Germans. Then it came to me, one of the great eye-openers of my life. If Germany and Austria were our enemies, then Bohemia was our enemy too. Here I was in a neighborhood filled with Bohemians and in Chicago that was filled with Bohunks, and yet I understood for the first time, in spite of the festivals, the polkas, the Sokols, and all the rest, and even the language and newspapers, we weren't Bohemians anymore. We were Americans!

The war ended, and I was never called on to serve, and America won, and Bohemia wasn't a part of Austria no more. It was its own country, Czechoslovakia. The Czech flag was everywhere, but it never flew higher than the American flag. Even though people felt pretty good about Prague being the capital of a country, it didn't mean 1919 was a good year. The bad stuff just kept happening. That's when the flu started up.[37] People were dropping like flies. Mostly the young got it, so I wondered whether I'd join Stella. I still remember kids singing while they skipped rope:

"I had a little bird
Its name was Enza
I opened the window
And in flu-enza"

They say the flu bug got the young people the most, but I never got it. Ain't that the way it is? I never missed a sickness when I was a kid—measles, mumps, chicken pox, and I even had my ass kicked by whooping cough. But I never got the flu. Ma and Pa never took me to the doctor with those other sicknesses because it was so expensive. Pa called doctors, "Quacks" meaning they didn't do nothing to help, but it was really an excuse not to spend the money. Ma had some home remedies. I dreaded those more than being sick. She used to hang garlic around my neck and smear my chest with mustard. Pa used to give me a shot of blackberry brandy and then mutter that I was "faking it." What, did I invent the chicken pox bumps?

Well, one night Pa was sitting at the dining room table playing solitaire and moaning about something or other at work. Pa had that pissed-off look he got when you disturbed his concentration. Ma was screaming about not having enough money. Pa had his usual stub of a cigar in his mouth, and then I saw him suddenly take it out, sneer at it, then put that three inches of turd in the ash tray. "This cigar ain't worth shit," he says to no one in particular, so he goes back to his game of solitaire, and Ma goes back to her sport, busting Pa's chops about money.

Well, I go about my own business. I was making an onion sandwich, which was something a lot of folks ate in the neighborhood. You take a thick slice of some good heavy rye bread, spread some unsalted butter nice and thick on it, stick a big slice of raw sweet Bermuda onion on the butter, and shake salt and pepper on the top. I was about to put the bread in my mouth when Pa says, "I feel like shit. I'm going to bed." That stopped my hand halfway to my mouth, and Ma shut up. Pa never went to bed before us.

I'm not sure what time it was, but it was far in the night when I heard Ma and Pa through the wall:

"I ain't going to work," Pa says.

And Ma says back, "Whataya mean you ain't going? They'll dock you."

"I couldn't give a shit."

"I ain't making you breakfast then."

"I don't give a shit."

By the time I got dressed and drank my coffee the next morning, Pa was in a bad way. Even Ma seemed worried. She whispered to me. "He's burning up."

I was afraid to ask if Ma thought it was the flu bug. I went off to work and could barely make it through the day 'cause I was so worried. I don't even remember if I could eat my lunch. When the quitting whistle blew I ran home. As soon as I got to Pa and Ma's bedroom I knew things had turned worse. Pa was working hard to breathe. Ma said his lungs were filled up. His eyes were open, but he wasn't looking at anything.

Finally, I convinced Ma to let me get a doctor. I ran like hell, but doctors were pretty busy just then. It took maybe two hours before one showed up looking tired and beat up at the front door. I kinda remember his name, Kopek I think. He goes straight away into the bedroom, and Pa speaks up for the first time since I came home. "I don't want no quacks!" But the doctor ignores Pa, and Pa didn't have the strength to resist.

Ma screams at Pa, "You silly goose. Shut up and let Doctor Kopek examine you."

So Kopek unbuttons Pa's pajamas, you could see they were soaked, and he puts his listening thing with them hoses attached to Pa's chest. He puts it a couple of places, and I was so nervous I couldn't breathe. Kopek had absolutely no expression on his mug. Then he takes Pa's pulse and checks it with his gold pocket watch. It looked like a nice watch. It was so quiet I could hear that watch beating a rhythm from the other side of the room.

Doctor Kopek signals to us to come out of the room. When he's in the front room, he takes off his wire glasses and wipes them with a handkerchief. He asks Ma, "Your husband a Catholic?"

Ma gives him one of her special looks and says—and I can remember like yesterday—"Catholic? He's no Catholic, he's a Socialist, that's what he is," and then she crosses herself like she was playing a part in a Sokol play, "Socialists don't believe in God, and that's a mortal sin."

The doctor doesn't react one way or another and says something like, "Be that as it may, I thought if he were, then this would be the proper time to have a priest come to administer Last Rites."

I don't think Ma got it, but I sure as hell did. Ma asks, "So what's he got Doctor?"

"The flu," and he puts his glasses back on and adjusts them on his ears, "but there's nothing to be done because…"

"Nothing," she says, "You think I'm paying you five dollars to do nothing?"

"Madame, there are many people in need. You pay five dollars for my time. You, after all, called for me."

"I didn't call for you, my goose of a son called for you."

The doctor didn't say another word. He closed up his black case that looked a little like a clarinet case and walked quietly out the door. With that Ma shrieks, "Pa's dying! My Pa's dying." She collapses on the floor. I don't know if she really fainted or faked it. I can tell you she got up pretty damn fast when I splashed cold water in her face. She no sooner gets up then we hear this horrible cough come from the bedroom, and the two of us rush in. Ma's shrieking must have scared him. There's spit and blood, and the air pours outta Pa like it was coming out of a tire. And there was nothing to be done. Ma could shriek all she wanted. That was it. My Pa's life ended with no drum roll, no sweet song, no hymn.

Ma goes nuts. I try to calm her down, but she pushed me away like I was a toy. She starts pulling her hair and running around in circles. I got out of there and headed over to the parish. It was the only place I could think to go. The cool quiet—you ever hear Sonny Rollins[38] on the sax? The wax smell and incense, the statues. I needed it all right then. No street noise came in. The eyes of the statues all seemed to be looking at me. If anybody came in to light a candle or pray, every sound made an echo. It was then, without making any sound, the tears started pouring down my face, and I didn't care. The tears wouldn't stop, and it wasn't only because of Pa.

Some have said to me, "Don't tell me there's a God. How could a God that loves you let your Pa die, or Stella, or let the Eastland sink?" I don't know. I'll leave that to the smarter assholes of this earth. See, I know my Ma is right, I am a goose a lot of the time, so it's not my place to hand out advice, but I tell you this, if you open your heart, it's not emptiness that comes in. Mostly, I realized just then, the tears were not so much coming from the sadness and bad things around me, but the song that came into my heart. It was a song that became part of my music.

I've heard in the neighborhood about the whiskey priests and the priest caught with a hooker. Pa told the story about some priest having his way with a nun. I heard about how the church was stealing from the poor with their expensive statues and such. That's about people and buildings and people being people, the way they've always been. When I walked into that church and sat there what I got had nothing to do with them things. It was personal. All I know is if I hadn't gotten that song I couldn't have gone on then or plenty of times since. After all these years, I understand what Pa's problem was, why he was always angry, why he saw everything as "shit", why he was always fighting the bosses, the unions, the Church—Pa never surrendered. He kept his heart locked.

Chapter 7

Out of the Darkness Came Light

Even though Pa died in the summer, 1919 wasn't through with me. In the hot nights after he died I got in the habit of going for long walks that took me all over the city. When you're lonely and hurt, Chicago is the back-beat of your mood as you walk. The long dark viaducts, the coal yards, the blue electric flashes of the streetcars, the empty factories, and the heat lightning—quite a musical arrangement, the city jamming. Every now and then I caught a whiff of Lake Michigan or the Union Stockyards. Mostly, the city was mercifully quiet in the places I walked.

Then things changed on a dime. Looking back, I realize it couldn't have been more than a few weeks after Pa passed away. The Colored rioted.[39] Everywhere I could hear the bells on the Paddy Wagons roaring down the main roads. The riots were front-page news in all the papers. Finally, the governor brought in troops.[40]

The riots didn't stop me from walking. Walking was the thing that kept me put together. There were soldiers standing guard on some of the street corners with bayonets attached to their long rifles. Mostly, they ignored me or gave a look like they were bored. The flat helmets they wore looked uncomfortable and a lot of them wore their helmets cockeyed. Maybe that was more comfortable. One time there were two soldiers and their boss, a sergeant I suppose. The sergeant had a pistol strapped to his waist and a whistle hanging on his chest. So I guess the whistle made him important.

The sergeant sees me coming and says, "Hey pal, you know where you're going?"

I look up. I was surprised somebody talked to me. "Who me?"

"Who else? You see anybody else walking around?"

I looked around, "Guess not."

"Guess not," he says. I remember the smile on his face twisted down so you didn't know if he was laughing or angry. "We got us a beaut, boys," speaking to the two soldiers with rifles. "You hear about the riots?"

"Sure I heard."

"You keep going the direction you're headed, you're gonna get your head stove in with a brick."

"Really?"

"Yeah, really pal, cross my heart and hope to die."

"I guess I'll change directions then," I says.

"Now you're thinking."

"What way's safe?"

"Any way but this way."

So without saying another word, I just turned around and walked off in a different direction. I heard the three of them laughing when I walked off. Usually, I had a pretty good sense of direction when I walked, but I got myself turned around pretty good. I found myself along some railroad tracks near the stockyards. I figured that by the smell in the air, sharp acid and sweet manure smell all mixed together. I heard more police bells way off somewhere.

All of a sudden there's a gang of about twelve white guys in front of me. As soon as they talked I knew they were Irishers. Irish lived behind the stockyards.

"Hey, where you going so fast, boy?" One of them shouts out who's in the lead of the pack. All the rest of them hurry to catch up.

"Going for a walk."

"Going fer a walk are ya?" he says back in his Irish way and then talks over his shoulder. "Hey lads he's going for a walk." These guys all start laughing. I see one of them kicking a half brick loose from a pile of stuff. He starts hefting it in his hand, measuring it, weighing it. I start to walk away real slow. Out of the corner of my eye I see this brick whistling at me. I just had time to turn my head and kinda block it with my arm. It ricocheted off. Made my forearm hurt like hell, and it tore my shirtsleeve. "What did yuz do that for?"

Now these guys were all around me. "Will you listen Billy to that voice," the leader says to one of the guys in the pack, "sounds like one of them Polacks[41] or something."

"Maybe he's a nigger lover then, Sean."

"Maybe Billy, maybe he is. You a nigger lover Polack?"

I tell them straight off, "I'm no Polack."

And this guy comes back with, "But I got the nigger lover part right, didn't I? With the puss you got, what the hell kinda bloody animal are you?"

I denied I was a nigger lover. "I'm on your side," I said. It was a long time after that that I was able to look a Negro man in the eye having denied them once by saying I was against them.

"Is that a joke, lad?" Now I was completely surrounded. A couple of the gang was standing right over the track, and they start picking up the stones from the track bed and lobbing them at me. Most of the stones bounced off my back, but a couple landed on my head. One grazed my forehead, and I felt a trickle of sweat or blood, but when I wiped it, I knew it was blood.

One of them says, "I thought a Polack's head was made outta rock."

"I'm a Bohemian-American," I answered back.

"Great then. Careful lads, stand back, that means his head's made outta shit, but I think you're still a nigger lover."

"I'm no nigger lover." I did it again.

Next thing I know a stone bounces off my head and hits this guy Sean in the face. "Watch where you're throwing them rocks Brian, or I'll shove that fooking rock down your bloody throat."

"Sorry Sean," from somebody behind me.

"So you headed to help your nigger brothers?"

"I already said I was out for a walk. I got nothing to do with them people. They don't mean nothing to me." Three times I did it.

Somebody says, "Sean, what are we playing around with this nigger lover for? Let's teach him a good lesson then."

"Well I'll tell ya, Bohunk. You stay outta our neighborhood. Since you don't look too bright, I'm gonna give you a little reminder so you won't forget. Take him boys."

They were on me like a pack of hungry stray dogs. I got hit and kicked everywhere. I closed my eyes tight. The pain spun right up my spine like a cat climbing a tree. Don't know how long it lasted, but I got knocked unconscious. I come around, and the gang was gone, but the world was swirling, and spots of light were exploding in front of my eyes. With some effort I got myself sitting up and then I pulled my knees up. For a long time I sat there with my head on my knees. At some point I puked, but I didn't feel no better after. Finally, 'cause I was worried they'd come back this way, I got myself up, wobbly for sure.

Somehow, I wandered back to the neighborhood. It was a miracle 'cause I was damn groggy, and I don't remember a thing about the walk. The first gray light of morning already lit my way when I made it back to familiar streets. The roosters people kept in the backyard coops crowed. Dogs barked. The new day started, but I felt I belonged to yesterday.

When I came into the dark house it looked, if not different, then as if I hadn't been there in a long time, like maybe the way you feel after you get back from a long road trip. There was Ma snoring. The big kitchen clock was pushing on. I saw lumps of fresh bread under towels on the kitchen counter. Still I wasn't sure it was my house.

In the bathroom I held myself up on the edge of the sink and looked in the mirror. All around the edge of what I could see was fuzzy. There was a big knot on the side of my head. My eyes were swelled up, and there was dried blood and dirt all over my face. My nose was clogged up with dried blood. The earwax seemed pounded out of my head. I worked warm water and soap into the mess. The sink was so dirty from it I decided to take a quick bath even if the water was mostly cold. I had to get to work or I'd be canned, and I didn't want Ma to see me like this. I'll tell ya, I got scared when I took a leak. Mostly blood I'll tell ya. Ma had enough problems and was crying for Pa every night as it was. I didn't need her worrying about me.

I guess I'm a tough Bohunk 'cause I got myself together and made it to my place on the production line by the time the whistle blew. I didn't have any lunch with me. It was going to be a long day. The foreman and everybody else took one look at me and said things like, "Whew, what happened to you? You get run over by a horse?"

By 10 a.m. I was seeing double. No wonder I made a mistake, sending two parts down the wrong way on the production line. They had to stop the line. I could hear a manager hollering from fifty feet away. The foreman comes over to me and whispers in my ear, "George, get the hell home. I'm docking you today's pay. Get some rest. See a doctor for Chrissakes. You pull something like this tomorrow, you're off the job, got it?" Of course I got it. The only reason I didn't get fired is the foreman was an old beer-drinking buddy of Pa.

Ma was at work by the time I got home. I heated up some oxtail soup, which hit the spot. Then I turned in. I slept till my alarm woke me the next morning. I was stiffer than yesterday, but I thought my head was clearer. At least I felt rested, but when I stood up, I was still dizzy, and everything around was like a fuzzy ring. I had to get to work though. It wasn't like today back then. No sick days back then and no medical insurance. You wanted a job then you showed up to work. But things didn't get better. I kept confusing things. By the afternoon, I was walking home without a job. I got dizzy and damn near wandered into traffic.

Well Ma didn't figure nothing out until she asked for my pay envelope on Friday. I don't know how she missed the bruises.

"Where's your pay?"

"Got fired, Ma."

"Got fired. Jesus Mary and Holy Saint Joseph! Fired for Chrissakes! Now what am I going to do, huh? Ain't it bad enough without Pa's pay? We'll be living on the streets!" Then she starts bawling just like she used to do with Pa. I went out 'cause I couldn't stand it. I went to the church, but they were having some kind of praying thing like Stations of the Cross, so I went for a walk. I walked around the old school and wondered if Miss Stepanek was still there. I prayed God would bless her. If I ever made a million bucks, I'd give her a big chunk of it.

For a week the days wandered up and down the scales in no particular way. I slept late even though Ma yelled at me and called me a "lazy goose" for doing nothing but going on walks. Slowly, one half note at a time, I got better, but if I twisted my head real fast the stars started all over again. One night I didn't feel tired no more, so I left the house and went walking. I walked and walked. It was a rainy night and the clouds hung low. I looked over my shoulder and saw the lights of downtown bouncing off the clouds. I knew I was walking south and east. Then up ahead, I saw something going on—lots of lights, some honking horns, people out on the street.

I walked toward the lights the way a bug flies to light on a summer night. Just then, I had a wish to be around people. It had been a long time since I felt that way, and the activity put a little spring in my steps. Maybe I even smiled.

I was on the back side of a place. No windows were open, and the doors were shut. The outside lights were on the other side of the building. In the shadows I saw a man lying hunched over against the wall of the building. Maybe he was drunk or dead, but that isn't what caused me to stop in my tracks. Coming through the walls was something I'd never heard before and froze me to my spot on earth as if that July night had turned to winter. It was a cornet and clarinet and piano and maybe other instruments. It was crazy, and it was wild, and it was hot. It rolled through my gut and weakened my knees. It was what a short time later I'd come to know as jazz. It covered up every numb spot inside me. It was a jigger of rye and the sweet perfume of a gal next to me.

When I came to again, only one thought crossed my mind—get inside this building and find out who or what was making this music. I ran to the front of the building from the alley. The other side was a different world: full of lights, laughing people, men and women kissing in the street, yelling, and then some guy comes up to me and asks me if I want to buy a bottle of booze for a buck. I guess this guy hadn't heard about prohibition. But I wasn't interested in booze or the lights or anything else just then. I wanted that music.

The name of the joint was the Highlight Café.[42] They let me in, but they gave me a looking over. I wasn't dressed like the swells in the club, so they let me stand in the back and nurse a beer. No drinking was allowed because of Prohibition, but nobody seemed to notice. They didn't care if I was still a kid. The booze was flowing. I think the guy who let me in, a Negro I got to know later, took pity on my poor ass. He could see what the music was doing to me, and I know, because we talked long hours about it later 'cause it got to him too.

He was a good kid, and he was square. When we talked, we understood each other even if our skin was different. He played the clarinet in the style of Sydney Bechet. Both of us listened to Bechet together when he was in Chicago. We cleaned floors in some club just to be able to listen. Bechet was a master. This kid, his name was Wilson, was struck down but a few months later by crossfire in a mafia shoot-out about a block away from the Highlight. That was the end of a mighty fine clarinetist, good young man, and my first Negro friend. He didn't even get a mention in the papers. But he was gone, and even though I knew he was gone, I'd look for him at the clubs for a long time after. A friend don't just disappear from your mind. His real name wasn't Wilson, but he never told me his real name. He called himself Wilson after President Wilson because he said, "The President was a man of peace." Those were tough times, and prohibition was making people crazy. And you know, at night sometimes when I'm alone, and my own death is on my mind, thoughts of Wilson come back to me. I still miss him.

Well I stood there in the back of the Highlight that first night sucking this music into every corner of my body. The crust of sadness of the last few years started to break off me like chunks of dried and cracked paint. I remember hearing a jazzed up version of the World War I song, *How Ya Gonna Keep 'em Down on the Farm After They Seen Paree*. People were laughing and dancing. You couldn't keep your legs still. Kryl had never dreamed music could sound like this.

Well I learned just how lucky I was. It was maybe the most famous jazz band of the time called the Creole Jazz Band[43] that came up the river[44] from New Orleans. The big bald-headed guy leading it was none other than Joseph "King" Oliver. He played cornet. Yes cornet. My instrument! This was the band Louie Armstrong[45] got his big start with and one of his future wives, Lil Hardin, was a piano player with them. She was a pretty picture.

Let me tell you about jazz and color. We that were in jazz weren't bothered by color. What we cared about was how you handled your instrument. I learned from the black man, and I jammed with them after hours when no one was around to bother us about color. At the same time I had to live two lives. I couldn't tell anybody at the factory in my next job or in the neighborhood that I thought Lil Hardin was pretty. You had to mind your P's and Q's. I had to learn to have separate emotions. Things that were funny in one place weren't funny in the other. I can't tell you how many times on lunch break or over a beer on payday some guy talked about how disgusting the idea of kissing a Negro was or how low it would be to marry a "Dago." I laughed at the jokes and often the same night, after hours, I'd be filling in or jamming with a band that was all Negro. I can only say the jokes made me feel uneasy, but the music we made put me at peace.

Now I see the black man isn't putting up with the way things have been. There's that woman down in Alabama who wouldn't give up her bus seat to a white man.[46] I saw it on the TV at the bar. They got a boycott and people are protesting. One guy at the bar said they should have dropped an atomic bomb on the boycotters. Another guy told the bartender to "turn that shit off." Some other guys said, "They better keep away from Cicero." God almighty, it takes your breath away. I hope colored folk get their rights.

Some still say that Jazz is a Negro music. Only the Negro can play jazz. They say it's in their blood like the way a Bohemian can play polka. Music doesn't have rules like that. Still there's no denying, in the beginning it was the Negroes who were the best. The white guys basically tried to copy those Negro guys. It's what I did too. The Negro musicians from New Orleans set the bar way up high.

In those early years, there was mostly two styles, a salt style and a pepper style. My friend, Bix Beiderbecke, went a long way to changing that, but I want to talk about that later. Some of us were lucky to learn and play in both groups, but for the most part, the bands didn't mix officially. There were Negro bands and white bands. In Chicago, a lot of the white bands played up on the north side. And then when the record contracts started, the white guys seemed to get most of the breaks. A lot of the Negroes got sore about that. It seemed even in jazz the odds were stacked against them. And they are the ones that gave jazz to America.

For me, that evening listening to King Oliver was a whole new start. The cobwebs cleared. That music was the only thing I wanted in life. It was like God came down and told me, "This is what I want you to do. Go blow that horn of yours. Blow them walls down." The next morning I took the silver and brass polish to that Conn, and I lubricated the valves too. For a long time I held my cornet without doing anything but taking the time to admire it.

Chapter 8

Leading a Double Life

My uncle Tomas came through for me and found me another factory job at the Chicago Screw and Bolt Company on the west side, and not too far a streetcar ride from the Cicero house. Uncle Tomas was a successful guy. His wife, Estelle, smelled of lilacs. It was Uncle Tomas who had taught me to "keep my nose clean, work hard, and you'll get your fair share." Tomas and Estelle both worked hard. They didn't have no kids, but they had a cabin up in the north woods of Wisconsin. They went there every summer for two weeks. Sometimes they rented it out and made more dough that way. I began to think it would be nice to have a cabin in the north woods, too, and fish for Muskie and Walleye Pike like Uncle Tomas did. Uncle Tomas wore a tie every Sunday. He wanted to be seen as something respectable, not like some working stiff. Some people said he put on "notions."

The factory work wasn't hard, but I got to tell you, I got confused a lot, not bad enough to get sacked, but my head still didn't work right. I didn't see double no more, but something wasn't right. Bright light really bothered me. Later on as a jazz musician I was one of the first to go on stage wearing shades. I didn't do it to be cool. It helped with the light.

I had a friend at the factory named Jimmy Nosek, and I told him I thought my brain got scrambled when them Micks beat on me. So he holds up two fingers and asks me how many fingers he's got up, and I tell him two, and he tells me not to worry.

Then just to be sure he says, "Follow my fingers with your eyes." He moves his fingers from one side to the other in front of my face. I do as he says, and he says back, "You handled it like a champ."

I asked him where he learned that, and he said he learned it in the "fight game." Seemed Jimmy had worked for a few years at a Chicago gym. Sometimes he even worked as a corner man for some pretty handy kids. "You're alright sport," he says to me. "A couple of pops to the head never hurt nobody."

Sometimes when we had nothing better to do late at night, Jimmy and I used to cool our heels over at a diner on what is now called Cermak Avenue. See, Cermak was the Mayor of Chicago, and he took a bullet for President Roosevelt, so they named the street after him.[47] All the Bohemians in the world were proud of him because Cermak is a Bohemian name. Back then, they just called it 22nd Street.

It was hard to keep quiet about my music. The fellas at the plant would laugh if I said anything, and the part about playing with Negroes, I didn't even want to think about what they'd do. I needed my job. You don't go playing no improvisation when ya got to put food on the table, and Ma needed the help. At that point in my career, I wasn't thinking about quitting my day job. Still, I was busting to tell people the one thing in my life that sky rocketed my spirits and I know this sounds crazy, but protected my soul. I figured I could tell Jimmy, and he'd keep it under his hat. I figured except for Jimmy nobody I knew outside of the bands at speakeasies could understand.

So this one night I planned on telling Jimmy. He was always asking where I went so late at night. He deserved an honest answer. We decided to go to Zeke's diner just off 22nd. At night it was the only bright spot around. Its light spilled out onto the sidewalk the way the music did from Kryl's apartment. Sitting on a counter stool at night and looking outside, all you'd see were outlines of buildings and a security screen or two. Not a light was on outside. It was like being on a lit up stage in an empty club. The joint had the only color I could see, the only place with details. It was not a place you normally set out for. It was a place you ended up after you'd been some place.

It was clean and warm in the winter, and a big ceiling fan kept it cool in the summer. For a dime you got all the coffee you could drink. I hear in the old country you can sit in a café all night if you want. Not in Chicago. Time's money and money's time is the way it goes, but Zeke the counter man and owner liked to gas on with customers, so he didn't care. I wonder how many cups of coffee I've drunk from those white mugs in Zeke's joint. Up close the mugs have small little cracks like red veins in tired eyeballs.

That night when we were crossing the street, there were some guys passing out handbills on the corner. "Here you go brother, read and learn," one says as he hands us each one of the sheets. I see he's wearing a red ribbon on his lapel. Looking down at the print I see in big letters across the top, "WORKERS UNITE!"

"So what are you selling, pal?" Jimmy asks these guys.

"We're not selling anything. We're trying to stop something."

"And what would that be?" Jimmy asks back.

"We want to stop workers from being exploited by the fat cats."

"You don't say," I remember Jimmy saying that with that smile he used to get. "Think you can squeeze some higher wages out of them?"

"We want everybody to get the same. Nobody gets more than the next man."

"What makes you think I don't want more than the next man?"

"The workers have been stepped on. It's time the worker had a voice."

"I like that."

"Then take this and read about it." He hands Jimmy the paper, and Jimmy creases it down the center and puts it behind his pack of cigarettes in his shirt pocket. Like it was yesterday I can remember this conversation. My brain's like that. Sometimes I remember every detail, and then at other times, it's like somebody threw the switch and nothing stays.

Jimmy answers, "Well I'll tell ya what, you figure out how I can get one of those new bungalows they're building in Berwyn without robbing a bank to get the dough, and I'll join up." With that, we keep walking, and the guys on the corner just shook their heads.

We took a couple of stools at the end of the counter. Zeke was already drawing our cups of joe out of the big metal urns. Jimmy loaded his white mug with about three spoons full of sugar. I say to him, "Why don't you put some coffee in that sugar?"

"Real funny."

"Look at this guy, Zeke."

Zeke scratched his big cauliflower ear with a hand that was missing two fingers from a Hun grenade in the first World War. On his right forearm next to the mustard gas scars was a globe and anchor tattoo. He had been a Marine in the raggedy pants brigade[48]. He wore his white paper kitchen hat cocked on the side of his head just the way he wore his overseas cap in France. Zeke tells some stories about getting drunk on real French Champagne and about his Frenchie girlfriends, which I guess are about the most beautiful women in the world. Isn't that the way it is; you lose and you win.

"That Jimmy likes his sugar, don't he? If every customer was like Jimmy I'd go broke. So what are you boys up to?"

Jimmy answers, "Just cooling our heels, Zeke." A lady sat in one of the wooden booths along the plate glass front of the joint. She was dressed nice. No floozy or nothing. Her eyes looked like where I'd been on those walks behind the lights of the city, in those viaducts and behind the empty warehouses. For a second I thought of inviting her to join us, but then I thought the better of it. Didn't want to scare her. She'd left the dark for the light of Zeke's. Better to leave her alone with that. Sometimes that can be good enough. She had a gentle look that comes from being raised right if you know what I mean. My eyes kept turning her way. Lovely anything makes you do that. I've been known to stare at a flower or even the wallpaper behind the meat counter in Pavlacek's grocery for the same reason. Something about the barns and all, and the pretty trees. Or just try to keep your eyes off of Coltrane when he loses himself in his music.[49]

Just then the door to the diner opens and in walks the two guys that were passing out flyers on the corner. Zeke takes one look at them and says, "What do you two knuckleheads want?"

That kinda pulled those guys up short. The bigger of the two pipes up, "Well actually neighbor, we thought we'd give you a little business." They both looked like they could use a good meal.

"The kitchen's closed."

The shorter of the two gets huffy, "Hey whataya mean, pal? The sign says you're open."

Zeke leans on the counter. He had one of them chiseled jaws that let you know he meant business. "Not for Reds!"

The big one says plenty loud enough to the shorter guy, "Come on Stash, let's sit down. This mug can't just kick us out." So they plop themselves down at the other end of the counter.

With that Zeke reaches underneath the counter and pulls out the biggest horse cock I ever seen in my life. Them two guys' eyes got about big as saucers. Zeke starts taking a couple of steps in their direction and the both of them scram. When the door closes behind them, Zeke shakes his head, "Reds! I'm having nothing to do with them revolutionaries in my restaurant."

Jimmy adds his two cents. "They think they're gonna take over the world!"

"How about some more coffee boys?"

"Sure," we answer.

I glance over at the lady. She seems a little upset. I wanted to say something soothing to her. And then, just as Zeke is heading over to the urn to get our mugs refilled, and before I think of what to say to the lady, a house brick comes flying through the plate glass. Glass goes flying everywhere. The lady screams. I run over to her. She had a smooth pretty face, and now it's got a cut that's running all the way down her cheek. It's gonna leave a nasty scar. Me and Jimmy use some napkins to mop up the blood while Zeke goes outside to look for the beat cop. The poor lady is trembling, and I don't blame her much. We get her name and try to calm her down. Jimmy, if you can believe it, is holding her hand. He tells her it reminds him of being a corner man in the fight game. From what I know about dames, I don't think that's exactly what she wanted to hear.

We stay with Linda until the meat wagon gets there. The cop has a lot of questions. We figure it had to be the Reds that did it. Zeke boarded up the window but never closed. He said, "I ain't gonna be intimidated by Bolsheviks!"

And then what do you think happens? Jimmy tells me maybe a week later that on a hunch, just the way he plays the horses at Hawthorn Park,[50] he looks up Linda, and they hit it off. The lucky dog got married nine months later. Anyway, the point of this story is to explain that it wasn't easy to talk about my music. Nobody was in the mood for it that night. Maybe Linda coulda been. She seemed the type, but I guess I'll never know that. I talked about music when I was around musicians. And with *Stella by Starlight*, of course. I still talk with Stella about music. So my life was split right down the middle. Day was the factory and night was the music. For me, night was light and day was dark.

Chapter 9

Getting a Break, Sort Of

So it was the "Roaring Twenties", but I'll tell ya, nobody was wearing raccoon coats[51] in my neighborhood. Nobody was getting rich fast. Still, if you wanted a factory job, you had your pick. A lot of people want things instantly. "Elbow grease and the sweat on your brow," is what Uncle Tomas said you needed for success. It takes hard work to get somewhere. Nothing feels better than working for something. If you don't work hard, life is tasteless like potato knedliki without gravy. My bet is the first thing God asks when you die is, "Did you try?" So pay attention you young musicians out there. Be prepared to work and work some more.

Look it's not easy practicing after you're dead tired from a factory shift. At night I was in the clubs listening and learning. I called it night school. I don't ever remember saying to myself, "I made big progress today." Slow little steps that take a long time to add up, that's the ticket, like putting away a couple of bucks from your paycheck every week for a "rainy day fund". No sense pretending that progress that needs a magnifying glass to see is encouraging. On the factory line I see what I've done at the end of the day. There's a pile of nuts and bolts, but with the cornet, some days I swear I skidded backwards. But I put my shoulder into it. And when I made a mistake, I kept at it 'til I didn't make it no more.

Because of old man Kryl, I could read music. I had what they call a "classical background". That don't mean you could play jazz. Most of the fellas I knew or knew about, learned music by imitating what they heard. I did the same because when I started out, nobody was writing a musical score for what was being played. You had a few educational choices, listen to records, once jazz records started coming along, swallow your pride and jam with somebody better, or listen at night in the clubs. Listening was the word. So first there was the word or the sound, and from that came the light into your noggin', and you learned to play the light. From that light you made it your own—your own art, your own style. That's how we created something new from the words we listened to. For me, it led to the end of the rainbow. Lost count of how many phonograph records I wore out listening, taking in the word, waiting for the light to come, and then making it all new. The Austin High Gang[52] did it that way and so did Bix Beiderbecke.[53]

Over and over you listen to the solos. You learn your part, and you play along. For fun sometimes, you try to jazz it up in your own way. I spent every extra dime I had on jazz records. Okay, my clothes were worn out, but I had a phonograph, records, and a cornet. It was enough. For the first time since Stella had died, my heart sang with joy. I believed nothing less than God led me to jazz and that first club.

The bad things were there, but I mostly ignored them like the drunks and hookers at the clubs. Something new was shining inside me. I remember Easter that year 'cause it fit into the way I felt. Ma was even happy for once, dressed up, and drenched in sweet perfume. The whole neighborhood strutted out on the street going to Mass. Nobody looked sick. Everybody was glad as hell not to be at the plant. The air was damp but warm. The windows were open at home and at the church, too. My mood was like the last week of school. Near the altar were tulips all around the statue of the Blessed Virgin—purple, red, white. My eyes drank the color out of them. If I wasn't a jazz cornetist then I'd want to paint with bright colors. I'd try to make the picture alive just by colors.

Instead of screaming at us, which is what he usually did, the priest told us to be happy because we were saved. That's what jazz tells me. Be happy brother 'cause you're saved. Been resurrected. How could I be any other way than happy when I play jazz? Later, sitting in the front room after Mass still lives in my memory—the white curtains blowing, sometimes completely full, warm spring air coming in. Watched the curtains settle down and then blow and shake in syncopation, do a shimmy, and fill the dark front room with rhythm in white waves. I fell asleep watching them and then slept so deep I didn't know where I was when my eyes opened. Only when the train cars banged together in the rail yard did I figure out where I was.

I remember going into the kitchen a little hungry. We kept a jar of vanilla wafers. Back then, you bought vanilla wafers like dill pickles, from barrels. I took a handful from the jar and put them in a bowl and poured some nice cold milk over them, then I crushed them up so the milk and vanilla wafers became kind of a pudding or paste. It wasn't a Bohemian dessert, but it's always been my favorite. I guess it's an American poor man's dessert.

Turned out Ma landed a better paying job on the Western's swing shift, so I practiced while she was at work. When I wasn't practicing, I was at a cabaret listening. And when I wasn't doing neither of those things, I was dreaming about my music. The one problem I had was trying to figure out how I was doing. I'm told that's a big problem for all kinds of artists. Living with being unsure is a big part of the battle. And it's lonely. Really, to be lonely for a woman ain't in the same league.

One day I came out the back door by the kitchen to toss out the garbage. We wrapped the garbage in newspaper to keep the maggots away. Old man Czerny was outside fiddling with a hose. I had been practicing my cornet, and it came over me to ask him what he thought of my playing. I'd never asked anybody outright before. Czerny seemed like a square guy.

Just thinking about asking made my heart beat like in a bird I held once. I'd knocked the bird out of a tree with a stone. Yes, I did it on purpose I'm embarrassed to say. Don't know why I did that. All I can say is that when I was a boy I did such things. I picked the bird up 'cause I felt so sorry for it and responsible. It wasn't dead, only coal cocked. I knew that it was alive by its little heart beating. Finally, when it opened its eyes, I let it go. It flew off and rested on the power line. It looked back at me, but didn't say nothing. My heart was rap-tap-tapping just like that bird's when I asked Czerny.

So I call over to Czerny. "Say Czerny, what do you think of my cornet playing these days?"

His forehead gets all wrinkled, and then his face turns red as an August tomato. I guess the question tormented or embarrassed him somehow.

But hey, there's no reason for Czerny to feel that way, hell, we'd been next-door neighbors a long time. So I ask him again, "What do you think, really?"

"Get the hell outta here!" he says in a not too neighborly tone. Then he goes inside and slams the door.

Well, that's a Bohunk for you. It's hard to pin down a Bohunk. See, I figured I embarrassed him, so he ran inside to hide. So I say to myself, don't give up! I knocked on his kitchen screen door. Smelled like somebody inside was making drstkova polevka (tripe soup). Whew, that's one soup I can't get past the smell of. Anyway, we've been eyeballing each other most of our lives, least thing he can do is give me a fair answer to a straight question.

As I'm knocking, I see a shadow coming my way. It was the shadow that hung over Czerny. He lived with his older sister. Ma always said, "Czerny and his sister are just like the priests and the nuns." Everybody around said it, "There's more going on there than just living under the same roof." Ma tried never to say anything directly to them, and she made a sign of the cross if she passed them on the street. Ma could be subtle.

Finally, the shadow takes shape. It's what Jimmy called, "the seester with the big keester." She gets her nose right up to the screen and stares out beyond me, maybe all the way back to the chicken coops we all kept at the back of our lots. "Yeah what?"

"I'd like to ask your brother a question."

"Well, he ain't got time right now."

"Come on," I says back, "He left me on the edge, and I'd like to know what he thinks."

"Why don't you get off his back?"

"I'm not on anybody's back!"

Then from the back of the house I hear, "The hell you ain't!"

"See?" the sister says, raising her voice in an unlady-like way, "What did I tell ya?"

Well, I'm getting a little hot under the collar from the rudeness. So my voice probably wasn't the nicest and I say, "Look, I've been practicing my cornet a lot, and I know your brother hears me play. I just want an honest opinion about my playing."

"Is that all?" she says, raising her voice. "Hey Ervin," she calls back to her brother, "All he wants is an honest opinion." She looks me square in the eye, "I could give you that. I've been hearing you blowin' on that thing long enough."

"So whataya think?"

"I could fart better music."

Somehow I keep calm, and my reward was a beauty of a comeback. "I don't know if it would be better, but with that keester of yours, it'd be louder!" I turned on my heels and walked home. All the way back to the house I could hear her yelling every dirty word I ever heard at the plant and then some.

For a day after, every time I put my cornet to my lips I'd start giggling, thinking of the names she called me. Jimmy and Zeke laid down laughing when they heard the story. Zeke would stand back at the grill frying up a hamburger and start chuckling. "Tell me again what she said your male part was like—like a peanut was it?"

"From whacking off too much, she screamed."

And we went back and forth like that. Still, I can't hide how, for weeks after, I had no desire to play the cornet. Oh sure, I knew Czerny's sister was angry at the world, and who wouldn't be if the only thing you got keeping you warm at night was that moron brother, but the whole thing made me confused, and it made me ask myself about whether I was good enough for jazz. Not one concrete thing came to my mind about why it was right for me to be a jazzman. Sweat broke out on my forehead just thinking about it. Jazz wasn't paying a mortgage down or getting me a cabin in the north woods like Uncle Tomas. Seemed what I was trying to catch was gas, gas I couldn't smell or feel.

Things went bad to worse. When I'd normally be listening at a club, I was doing nothing more than staring at the kitchen wall, just the way Pa did sometimes. The more I stared the fewer answers I got, and the headaches were coming back from the beating them Micks gave me. I was looking for concrete, and there was just air. I prayed and tried to let God into the problem. I asked the priest, but he didn't want to talk about jazz. In the end I figured I was stupid.

Just about when I figured I was looking over the edge and going totally crazy, like a miracle, the doorbell clangs, and who's there but Uncle Tomas. Tomas was kind of an accomplished musician himself. He'd been playing the accordion all of his life and led a Bohemian polka band called "Tomas' Merry Makers". Tomas liked cigars, and he had one jammed in the corner of his mouth like Gus.

"George," he says, "How's your cornet playing coming along?"

"I'm not sure. I work hard and keep my nose clean."

"That's the spirit!" He drops himself on one of the kitchen chairs. I get him a cup of joe and a kolaczky, prune I think it was.

Tomas laughs in that kind of coughing laugh he had, like he couldn't let the laugh out and was pushing it out through too small a hole. "These are bakery kolaczky, aren't they?"

I told him, "Ano."

"Your old man couldn't stand your Ma's kolaczky, remember?"

"Yeah Uncle Tomas, I remember," I says back. But I didn't want to remember nothing about Pa right then. Some people like to talk about their dead relatives. Not me. Doesn't make me all soft. For me, I gotta pull my belt tight and think about that horizon that went as far as you could see when Ma and me worked on the onion farm.

"Oh Christ, how he used to complain! Like steel discs he called them. Needed a blowtorch to get through 'em. What a character your old man." Tomas picks his nose with his handkerchief and looks at what he pulled out for a while. "Hey George, I actually came here to talk about something serious."

I answer back, "I figured 'cause we're sitting in the kitchen." In our neighborhood, serious talks happened in the kitchen. If the stoves could talk…

"Look George," Tomas goes on, "You know I've been doing a fair business with my polka band. Lots of weddings, funerals, First Communions, church dances, you know what I mean. I don't get rich from it, but I take the money and sock it away. It adds up. I'm thinking of buying one of them Fords next year with what I've saved." He moves around on his seat, "Fact of the matter is I got problems with the band right now. Seems Laddy Popek has to quit because he's got some kind of tremor they call "Parson's Disease", so I'm wondering, 'cause I know you're playing that horn of yours all the time, think you could fill in for Laddy and play some tuba for me?"

"Tuba?"

"It's good money, and the girls like the traditional Bohemian costumes."

"Costumes! But I don't play tuba; I play cornet."

"I know that, but they're both brass instruments."

I answer with lots of hesitation, "Uncle Tomas, it's a different instrument. I don't know. I can't say I ever thought of playing tuba."

"Well if you can't, you can't," he comes back with. "But hey, I figured a favor to your favorite uncle, one musician to another. And don't forget, this is a chance to go professional."

"Uncle Tomas you done a lot for me. Lining up that job."

"Ah forget about it."

"No, I want to help you out, but I'm a jazzman." I forget if I actually said jazzman.

"Well kid, do you think if you aren't willing to give the tuba a try, you could at least do the tuba part with your cornet? See I got to have the rhythm."

"I suppose I could do that," I answer.

"That's the spirit! And I promise I'll use you as my number two trumpet."

"Promise?"

"If it ain't so may the good Lord give me a brain tumor. And hey, try out the tuba. It'll expand your horizons."

How could I let Uncle Tomas down? It's like Zeke: some days you get mustard gas, the next day you're rolling in the hay with some Parisian beauty. And so I learned the tuba, and I swear it helped my jazz. See, in polka you have your basic, oom-pah-pah. When I thought about it, I realized jazz has a lot to do with pah-dump-ah-dum. So I just had to twist things a little. It's all about syncopation, see. Sometimes I got solos on the cornet even if it made Uncle Tomas mad when I'd jazz up a polka.

I have good memories of helping Uncle Tomas out. It's a little embarrassing admitting how I played in a polka band. I can hear them Negro jazz musicians snickering at me and razzing me. But a gig is a gig, right? And yes, playing tuba when I was supposed to be a jazzman and an artist and all, okay I get it. I can laugh at myself, but I tell the story because I've learned how sometimes in the pauses in between the beats of life come some of the best times, and you get a lesson about what's important, even if it didn't figure in your plan.

Like it was yesterday, I remember playing in the Sokol Hall for a Saturday night wedding reception. It was the neighborhood Bohemian custom, and I think the Polacks did it too, to use a polka to get everybody to their dinner seats to kick off the evening. It's kind of a march. The bride and the groom lead it off. They lock arms and polka side by side with the close family right behind and then the other guests follow them in a long line. How pretty it looks from the band to see that pass by, the bride in her white dress, the young man trying not to be a boy, the generations skipping past, the friends, and the little kids not really knowing the dance but trying.

The way it started out was Tomas would announce the polka was about to begin by me blowing a big kind of jazzed-up bugle call on my cornet. Everybody in the place had their eyes on me. Then the polka actually started as everybody got lined up. I quick grabbed the tuba. There was yelping, laughing, and screaming. The polka got faster and faster. I couldn't believe old folks could move their legs so fast. When the bride and groom were finally at their seats in front of their plates, the music cut. Timing's everything in music.

The funerals were special too, but my heart won't let me talk about what I learned from them yet. Maybe someday, but not now. I don't know why that is so, but I can't hold off writing this book for that day to come. It will just have to have a hole in it like a stuck valve on a trumpet. Did you ever hear Sonny Clark's piano? That's the jazz that's on my mind right now. I'm hearing Sonny's *Deep in a Dream* on the *Leapin' and Lopin'* album.[54] Rest in peace Sonny.

Sometimes I picked up five bucks and once a sawbuck for those polka gigs. I wasn't going to save up enough for no automobile, but I did get a suit so I could look decent when I played jazz in the club. It felt good to get paid for the effort, and it taught me how to control the stage jitters.

Chapter 10

Bix Beiderbecke and What He Meant to My Life

People have said to me, "We are all the same down deep." I understand what they are trying to say. They mean we should be more brotherly because we all want the same things, and anyway, we all are sinners together. I understand, especially the sinner part. I've seen the darkness in people's eyes and looked in the mirror deep into my own and seen things that make me shake. Still, if you are like me you notice the differences between people right away. Take the New Orleans cornetists Emmet Hardy[55] and "Wingy" Manone.[56] Both were giants in early jazz, both knew their instruments inside and out, and both played a lot of the same songs. Hell, they came from the same town. Each had two eyes, one nose, two lips, well okay, in the case of "Wingy", one arm, but you get my point. You could say they were the same, but what came out of their horns was different. That difference came from deep locked-up parts of their hearts.

The heart is deep and strong and mysterious. Seen a jazzman's life a wreck from dames, ponies, booze, and dope, and still his heart explodes with music that brings you to tears. Each time he blows his horn or tickles those piano keys, something new gets born. When you work at the Western, nothing new gets born. You make new things, but they aren't really yours; and when they're all stacked up and lined up as far as the eye can see and even beyond where you can't see, so what?

Not too long ago, Junior[57] (can't remember the cat's last name), a fine percussionist though, I guess I'm getting old. Anyway, he was telling me over a Bud between sets in a gig he was playing with the Chicago bassist, Wilbur Ware, that "the heart's a two-way pump." Now see Junior was no doctor. What he was talking about was the discovering and the creating you get when you play jazz. The Bee Boppers[58] all get into the deep end of what jazz meant a lot more than us early guys, but the point he was making is true for somebody like King Oliver or any of the new jazzmen.

It took a while for what Junior said to sink in, but it's come to mean plenty to me. If you let it, original jazz, and that means the pure stuff, as pure as anything in nature like the soil Ma and I digged in for onions, can get pumped into your heart. Then, the next time you blow your horn and try for something that's yours and yours alone, it comes out better than you ever could imagine. It pumps in, and then something happens inside, and new gets pumped out. Then somebody hears your stuff, and it gets breathed into his heart, and then out comes something still newer. It's a rhythm this pumping—or is it breathing? Maybe it is breathing, but it's making new what wasn't there before. I love that about jazz.

I have a copy of Bix Beiderbecke's first record. It's a song called *Fidgety Feet*.[59] He did it in the early 1920s. And I have some other early recordings of his too like *Tia Juana*. He gave me that phonograph record as a present. Bix wanted to be liked. He always looked like a little kid dressed up in a monkey suit to me. I don't know why his parents didn't like him. I think he embarrassed them—the drinking and all. They spent a lot of money and time trying to give him a chance to live the straight and narrow, but nothing stuck. Look, I'm not taking anything away from the greats like Satchmo, Dizzy Gillespie, or this new kid Miles Davis, but I have to admit I pumped a lot of Bix into my heart. I think my soft tone is a little like Bix. It lets me get what jazzmen call "dissonance". Dissonance is a cornflower growing along the Western's brown brick wall.

At my age, I think a lot about Bix. I wish he wasn't gone. I've heard people say, if he'd done this or that, he would have been better, or more famous, or would've made more money. When I listen to *Fidgety Feet*, all I can say is, who cares? Sometimes lately, I think about dying, not in a sad way, I just think about it with not much more behind it than the thinking I give to whether I'll eat a prune or apricot kolaczky. I think about who I'll meet when I cross over the Jordan. Let me confess that I hope the first person I meet after Stella is Bix. Nothing could give me more pleasure than to see him standing there, called home to Jesus, with his cornet in one hand and flask in the other, waiting to welcome me and celebrate my coming over.

Still, I want to be honest here. I sigh to think about it. To put it down on paper weighs so much that the pen feels heavier than my cornet. For all the joy Bix brought into my life, there was a bad side for me too. I was under his spell, and he became an infection almost like the one that took Pa. Years after he died, I came to realize Bix took a lot of my blood but never gave it back. I don't mean the music but the blood and tears of everyday life. He drained me, plain and simple. And still, I want to see him when I die. Some Einstein out there can figure that out.

When I told him about Bix, Jimmy Nosek said, "Typical of a drunk." In fairness to his parents, when Bix got himself kicked out of that boarding school up north,[60] he was pissing on them too. Maybe they didn't understand his music, but they were trying to do right by him. Hell, if it wasn't for his mother introducing him to the piano when he was a little boy, I doubt he ever would have been a musician. Why do people spit on the folks who are trying to help them?

One evening I remember I was listening to a few sets at the Friar's Inn[61], and I look up at the band, and who's jamming with them, Bix! By the way, most people called him "Beiderbecke." He's up there on the bandstand wowing the crowd, and every second he's not blowing that cornet of his, he's smiling like a little boy with those big ears sticking out. The place went wild every time he soloed.

During a break I pushed my way up to him. We'd got acquainted 'cause we kept running into each other at the jazz clubs late at night. I was just a few years older than Bix, so it was easy for us to start jawing. For a moment he didn't see me, 'cause he was shouting to somebody, "Twenty-two skidoo! Twenty-two skidoo!"

"Bix, hey Bix, remember me?"

He blinks twice, rolls his eyeballs and says, "Georgey Porgey! How ya doin' pal?"

"Doing good, doing good," I answer back to him.

"Hey," he says back, "get up here and spell me a while, will ya?"

I laugh and wave my arms. "Me spell you?"

"You got your horn, don't ya?"

I couldn't lie to him. The black case for that silver Conn was right at my feet. I shrugged, "Sure I got it."

"Then get your ass up here."

The funny thing is, I obeyed him. The Friar's Inn was one of, if not the hottest, clubs in the whole damn city. I never thought I was ready to play there or any club the swells and gangsters went to. Never on my own or even if somebody else on that stage asked would I have climbed up there, but with Bix, see he was a real Pied Piper, I couldn't say no. He said, "Get up here," and I got up there.

No sooner do I get up there without a second to think about what the hell was happening than the guy on the clarinet, I don't even remember his name, says, "Ok let's go. *That's a Plenty*.[62]"

"*That's a Plenty*?"

"What are you deaf? You know it right?"

I did know it. I shook my head yes and he says, "Three four," and I started playing. I played out of pure instinct. Next thing I know Bix is standing next to me clapping his hands and saying to the folks in the club, "Hey, round of applause for my buddy Georgey Porgey."

Some thug of a guy at a table up close to the stage with a big cigar in his mouth shouts up, "Good job kid."

What a moment that was! Every nerve in my body was on fire. I wanted that feeling again. No moment in my life has put a smile on my face like that one. I remember once a fella telling me about a home run he hit in his first professional ballgame. After finishing that song, I understood him. Later, when I had a jazz band, I made *That's a Plenty*, our theme song.[63] Maybe it was Uncle Tomas who gave me a professional start in music, but it was Bix who launched me. After that, I practiced more and more, and I sat in every chance I could get, no matter the club, no matter the band. And the chances started coming my way.

I jammed. Baby I jammed! That's how you learn technique and your own style. I learned to change style to fit the band. I took every solo I could get, and I set up the other guys. That's one of the reasons I got invited to sit in. My reputation was that I wasn't trying to hog the song. I was respectful. I knew my place. Fitting in is something you gotta do. You young guys out there, you pay attention to what I'm saying. Nobody likes a show boater. And listen here, for you musicians who think you're the best to come along, there's always somebody better. Be humble.

It's like fighting. Over the years I can't tell you how many bar fights I've witnessed. Sometimes I've even had to throw a punch or two. Each time, some jackass gets the fight going because he thinks he's the toughest guy on the block. Nine times out of ten he gets his face shoved in and balls kicked for good measure.

The worst fight I ever saw wasn't in a club. Mostly at the clubs the people were just trying to have a nice time. Negroes got along with the "hambones" and vice versa. Music does that. I see the faces on the people when I'm playing. They think you can't see when you're up there on stage, but you do see. It's dark out there, and in the darkness the folks let their guard down. They take their masks off and show an emotion or two.

What a wonderful thing to have the chance to see that. You can walk on the street for ten years and never see it. People pass you on the street looking like they've been embalmed. When you see the people out there let their emotions go, it gives you a hint about how much people lock inside, but then again it also teaches about how wondrous and deep people feel. Though I don't have the words to explain it, seeing those people from the stage has made me proud to be a human being.

Anyway, the worst fight I seen had to be at a night game I went to at Comiskey Park. I forget who the White Sox were playing that night. I'm thinking it was the Detroit Tigers. You get out in the cheap seats, way out in left field, and the boys are drinking a beer an inning. That happened to be where I was sitting. Somebody in the upper deck pours a beer down on the heads of guys sitting on the first deck.

I must have been twenty rows back from those mugs that got hit with the beer, near the open archways that looked like big church windows running along the back of the park. Over the roar of the crowd 'cause Billie Pierce[64] or maybe Ted Lyons[65] just struck somebody out, I hear this guy scream, "Son of a bitch!" He looks up at the upper deck and shakes his fist. With that, it was like it was raining beer, and I heard every four-letter word invented in the English language.

A lot of the guys that got hit with the beer were from the Holy Name Society of some south side parish. I knew 'cause they had nametags saying it. They were really pissed since one of the priests who was sitting there got completely soaked. Well, the next thing you know, the Holy Name Society is rushing up the ramp to the upper deck. If I'm not mistaken, a priest was leading the charge. Go Father! Don't take crap off nobody!

It took about one minute for the fight to spread from the upper deck to the lower deck. It was like everybody was waiting for the moment. I was watching a tornado coming at me. I ducked down under the seats. My memory of that moment is as clear as anything in my life. I can still see the dirty concrete, some old smashed soda straw, three cigarette butts, one with a lipstick smudge, and two empty peanut shells. Nearby, I heard somebody fall and the wind blowing right out of him. The police were thick as flies—whistles blowing. At least I didn't get pinched. What a night!

CHAPTER 11

More About Bix

Anyway, back to Bix. When I first met him he was still doing time at that boarding school up north in Lake Forest. This may be the age of science, but I haven't heard a peep out of no scientist to explain why it is a family can live together and not have a clue of what makes each other tick. Bix's parents didn't know their own son's good heart. You know, it might have saved Bix if they had. How could they think a school could change what was on fire in him and make him into something they wanted? Nobody's got the right to do that, especially in America.

Bix in boarding school! Do you keep songbirds in a chicken coop? But you know, I have to admit we are all a little like Bix's parents. We don't bother to really know the people we are close to. When I think back on Pa, I remember some little pieces of advice like, "Get a trade so ya don't have to shovel shit for a living." His favorite meal must've been roast goose 'cause he didn't talk while he ate it. And I remember he wrote right-handed but put his belt to me with his left. Honestly, I couldn't tell you his favorite color or why he was a White Sox fan. He bellyached about politics, but I don't know if he voted. I don't know how he met Ma. Sometimes I wondered if I was really his boy.

One night I remember being out with Bix when he was still at the academy. We all jammed at a club that just opened. Never have I been so hopped up from nothing other than life. My shirt was drenched with sweat; every woman was beautiful; the fizzy burgundy tasted like French Champagne. Later, I told Jimmy and Zeke at the diner over a cup of joe, "Maybe you seen one of these here mad dogs that hangs around the rail yard chasing its tail. Well, if a tail had been dangling from me, I would've looked just like that."

After we jammed, we got a bottle. I took sips, but Bix drinks from it like it was lemon phosphate. We stopped at a place to eat, and I'm buying everybody food. I'm calling the waitress "doll". "Doll, how about getting us all a steak smothered in onions?" or "Say doll, when you get a break how about bringing us our check?" We started going to one cabaret after the next: The Savoy Ballroom, the Sunset Café on 35th and Calumet, even Freiburg's on 60th and Cottage Grove. I think it was the night we saw Johnny Dodds.[66] Don't recall if he was still playing with "King" Oliver at the time. What I especially remember about that night is that the wind was coming off the lake, and you could smell it. There was that line in a song back then: "Mississippi water tastes like turpentine but Lake Michigan water tastes like sherry wine."

I think it was at The Lincoln Gardens because in my mind I can see that big spinning glass ball they had hanging from the ceiling. Bix kept sluggin' down the booze, and he keeps shouting out things to the band. Now I knew they were encouragements, but see, his voice sounded drunk. Other customers start complaining. Next thing you know, Bix is in a shoving match with one of the waiters who had a physique like Johnny Weissmuller.[67] By the way, I knew Johnny a little bit. He was a Bohemian kid from Chicago. A nice guy. Anyway, I swallowed hard and got in between them. All Bix needed was to get his lips smashed by this gorilla. I told the waiter we didn't want no trouble and that I'd be responsible for Bix. Guess the waiter had more important things to do. There was a moment when he was going to take a poke at me, but then he let it go and said, "Get the hell outa here." I wrestled Bix outside.

Bix's school chums got sore. "What did you do that for Beiderbecke?"

"You coulda got us all kicked out of school."

"Piss on school," I remember Bix growling.

One of his chums said, "Well then piss on you."

They all took a powder and there I am with Bix, who's pickled and bent over the curb puking. Between heaves he's moaning, "Georgey Porgey, Georgey Porgey." Then he takes something out of his mouth and hands it to me. It was this false front tooth he had since he was a kid. I put it in my handkerchief and stuffed it in my pocket.

I saw a big clock on a bank building. I couldn't see my own watch 'cause it was underneath Bix's arm. It was 1:45. I let out a slow long breath. "Okay," I says,

"How do I get you back to that school of yours?" I knew it was far north, and I didn't have the cab fare, so I figured we'd better start walking and maybe Bix would sober up some, and we could figure out if we had the fare between us. So I threw Bix's left arm over my shoulder, and off we go, weaving down the street.

After walking to nowhere for a while, and getting there by the slowest pace you could think of, Bix perks up a little and he says clear as can be, "You know Georgey, you play as good as those stiffs we heard in the last joint." I remember the moment he said that. I was looking down the long street that seemed to go on almost forever. Way at the end to where I could see, the streetlights came together in a point where everything vanished. Not a car was on the street. All I heard was our shuffling feet beatin' a syncopated rhythm to the jazz playing in the back of my brain.

We kept walking and that vanishing point seemed to never get closer, like chasing a rainbow. Finally Bix tells me the school's in Lake Forest. He might as well have said, Iowa. But Bix had to get back. Finally, I see this cabby sitting behind the wheel with a light on reading a newspaper. I tap on the glass, and I tell him square, "Buddy, I don't have enough for the fare, but if you take my friend back to school, I'll give you my watch. It was a pretty cheap Elgin. He looks at the watch. I take it off, so he can examine it better.

"Ok kid, you're on, it's a slow night, but you're going along for the ride. I'm not taking responsibility for your pal even if it was a gold watch."

The ride took forever. I don't know if the driver and I spoke but a few sentences the whole time. Pretty much, Bix stayed passed out in the back. At least he didn't heave no more. At one point in the ride he kinda woke up. He starts showing me the fingering on one of his solos. He reached into his breast pocket, fiddles around for a while, and then hands me a bottle of trumpet valve oil. He says, "Here, Georgey, hold this a second." Then he goes back fishing around in the pocket but comes up with nothing and then forgets what he was looking for. He turns to me, and his face was as pale as the moon. "Georgey," he says, "I can't sit still." He sounded scared. "Whataya do when ya can't sit still?" and he started to cry. I answered to myself, "I don't know."

At the school, the cabby helped me drag Bix from the back and then says, "I gotta get back to town. Might as well have company. Dump your friend off, and I'll wait for ya, but for Chrissakes hurry up."

Lake Forest was like nothing that was part of real life. Even in the dark I could see the houses were castles with towers and gates and stuff. This is where the big shots lived. I think to myself maybe it was like where Ma came from in Krumlov 'cause they had a castle there. Anyway, I got Bix to his room without a problem and put him to bed. I put his horn case under his bed and my handkerchief with his tooth under his pillow. Walking back down the shiny hallways of that place, listening to my shoes click like an old grandfather's clock, I got the heebie-jeebies. Somehow I got the feeling I was seeing something I wasn't supposed to see, like spying on an undertaker doing a lady stiff.

Turns out the cabby was one swell guy. He took me all the way out to Cicero. With an orange sun coming up over the lake, I took him to Zeke's joint and bought him a breakfast and that pretty well cleaned out my pocket. When he left and I got to work, I discovered my watch in my jacket pocket. The cabby must have slipped it in when we was at Zeke's. He was a swell guy.

Over the years that ride and that cabby keep coming to mind, and yet, I don't recall his name. We gabbed the whole ride and then for another hour at Zeke's, and we woulda gone on gabbing but for the fact I had to get to work. He told me his old man had come back from the war missing two arms and couldn't work no more. They were a farming family from out west of the city along the Illinois River, which he said was as rich farmland as you can find. But they couldn't make a go of farming what with the father's situation. There were five kids, but he said one of three boys was no good, and his mother pretty much lost her mind over the situation. One of the daughters ran off with somebody, and they went out west, and the cabby don't know what happened to her. So they sold the farm that he said they grew corn and soybeans on and come to Chicago looking for steady work.

The cabby said his mother died of the influenza when it came around the second time. He said that really it was the city that killed her. But he said through it all, his father never stopped smiling. He said the remaining three children all pitched in and kept the father going with proper food and kept him clean and told funny stories to keep themselves together, and he was still living and never complaining. "Crazy," he said, "but he's happy." He said that, I remember.

I asked him, "How is it your old man can keep smiling?"

He scratched his head, and a bushy mop of hair he had. He looks at me long with as honest an eye as I have ever seen in a man, and he says, "I don't know."

After the cabby left, I sipped some more coffee with a minute or two to spare before I had to go. Zeke left me alone with my thoughts. I hung onto my stool until the sunlight came through the big plate glass windows of the joint. When I saw Marty Sedlacek pull the security gate back on his pawn shop, I knew it was time to leave and walk over and make some bolts and screws.

When I got to my work place and looked down the line, it reminded me of the street I dragged Bix down. The overhead lights, the conveyor belt, the skylights, the workers, everything vanished in a point, way out at the edge of where I could see.

CHAPTER 12

NOTHING SITS STILL

For some time in the twenties, when we were both in our twenties, Bix and I drifted apart, but not for personal reasons. Careers do that. There were his recordings with the Wolverines.[68] Then he was down in St. Louis for a while.[69] A lot was going on. I finally connected back up with Bix over one holiday weekend when I traveled up to Detroit and filled in a couple of evenings in the Jean Goldkette Band[70] "The Famous Fourteen" they called them. They were playing at one of the premier ballrooms of all times, the Graystone Ballroom. I never saw so many people dancing in one place before. Bix had fixed it up for me. Of course, he stole the show. If I was to bet, I'd bet Goldkette was a little uneasy with Bix. He wanted everything in the band buttoned down, but Bix was like trying to keep syrup in a sieve. Still, Goldkette was no fool; he knew talent.

Maybe on one side Goldkette was taking a chance with Bix, but on the other side, Bix took some heat for playing in the Goldkette Band on account of the fact that the band was a little too genteel and snooty. They smoothed out the jazz and orchestrated too much. Well, if you heard Bix's solos, then you'd close your yap on that score, even if he couldn't read music. Say what you want about that orchestra, it hatched all kinds of greats I had the pleasure to meet like Tommy Dorsey[71] and Hoagy Carmichael.[72] You can imagine what Hoagy's song, *Stardust*[73] means to me. I sing it all the time, even today. Stella comes alive each time. Her smooth cheek is against mine, and I smell that jasmine scent of hers.

"Sometimes I wonder why I spend the lonely nights
Dreaming of a song
The melody haunts my reverie
And I am once again with you
When our love was new

And each kiss an inspiration
Ah but that was long ago
Now my consolation is in the stardust of a song."

I tried to keep Bix's drinking down, but when I did, he'd give me this face and say something like, "Quit trying to act like my old man, Georgey." Lots of people tried to keep his drinking down. We had some good talks in those days. One night a couple of hours before the sun came up, we were sitting in a hotel room in some postage stamp burg in Illinois. We'd played together earlier. The hotel's back end was flush up against a field of ripening corn. It was August, and the room window was wide open. A breeze brought in the smell of the candy sweet corn and damp ground. The dirt smell reminded me of the prairie dirt I dug out back in the neighborhood and on one the onion farms. I figured I was smelling something that cabby knew well. I recall looking out the window. In the dark I could still see three or four rows of the stiff tall cornstalks with their tassels twitching in the breeze. Even though I couldn't see them, I knew those rows of corn went on forever maybe even beyond the edge of the earth for all I knew.

Only a small light was on in the room. Bix's head was half in and half out of the orange light. The part that was in a shadow was so dark I could barely see his eye. He was settled back in an easy chair, and his horn was taking five on the bed.

Bix was sober, and we talked about music. Bix had learned about European composers like DeBussy and Ravel. I told him about Kryl and Stella and what I knew of those composers. Stella, "my dream" I used to say. Now she was starlight. Not strong enough to make a shadow but out there forever for me to see. We talked about music, or music talked to us. Our hands held imaginary instruments that night. Making music nobody else heard. Fingering the keys and playing the notes. We dreamed about tomorrow, but we couldn't really see what was to come. Bix was ahead of his time, but he couldn't have imagined the Bee Boppers. If we could have seen tomorrow, would we have stopped right then and there? Sometimes I don't know what note is going to get blown out of my horn.

I got to admit that I came damn close to quitting my cornet after listening to Bix play. He was so good. I figured, what's the point? You listen to the giants like Miles and "Dizzy".[74] You know in your heart that they belong to a different club. But then I ask myself, so if I don't play, then what? What does God want me to do with my life different? No answers come.

God has a way of not answering those questions straight out. God would be a helluva poker player. Then, who knows, weeks later, one morning I'm crawling out of bed after a bad night. I could still hear Pa from long ago saying, "I feel like shit," and I knew what he meant just then. On the way to take a leak, I damn near tripped over the case to my Conn and stubbed my big toe doing it. Cussing and swearing, I limped into the bathroom. Then it just came to me, standing there dizzy in front of the toilet, a sad sight if there ever was one. I'm just supposed to do the best with what I got. That's good enough.

One afternoon Bix comes to me and says, "Hey Georgey, I'm going with Goldkette's boys out to New York. Jean thinks you could fill in. No regular offer but hey…New York. It's where jazz is going Georgey. Make a connection."[75]

"Leave Chicago? Permanently?"

"What the hell? Life comes around once, Georgey."

But who was going to take care of Ma? Seemed every week she had a new disease. And I had a good factory job. What would Uncle Tomas say? I didn't leave. What was wrong with the Chicago jazz scene anyway? The next thing you know, there I was at the LaSalle Street Station seeing Bix off. He was getting the red carpet treatment on the Twentieth Century Limited[76]. And just like that, Bix chug chugged his way out of my life, a red dot of light pulling away. I'd be lying if I told you life didn't seem empty for a while. Another memory of him has stayed with me still. There I was one night, playing some place, and I spelled Bix so he could get himself some fresh air. Rather than my Conn, Bix sticks his horn in my hand. Around the valves it was warm from his life. Metal doesn't hold warmth for long. Bix could set a room on fire by just the way he moved, flapping around like a blackbird learning to fly. Bix touched every piece of my body with music and made it explode, sending me in places I never thought you could go. But Bix, he was over me, and I was under him. There was something about that. It was too much like home. I remember I set his horn down respectful like and picked mine up.

Well, I still had my Conn, and the starlight above kept me going. That doesn't mean that I haven't kept asking myself ever since, what woulda happened if I'd gone to New York? Strange, Bix didn't make it two years. Oh, his playing was great I hear, but the booze killed him. Heard he went mad at the end. I'm glad I missed that. Years later I was doing a gig in Davenport, Iowa, Bix's hometown. I wanted to see the house where he grew up. So I ask a cop on the street if he could direct me to the Beiderbecke house. He says to me, "I don't know no Beiderbeckes."

Can you imagine that? One of the most famous people to ever come from that burg. So I say back, "But Beiderbecke is famous."

"Still never heard of him." He sends me off to a city building.

Some mug tells me, "Oh sure, I know where Beiderbecke, that drunk, resides." So he excuses himself a minute. Checks some book or another and comes back with a slip of paper. On it he's got an address scribbled down.

I thank the guy and head to the address. Real funny. The address turned out to be the Oakdale Cemetery. I found Bix's stone. August 6, 1931.[77] That was the date he died. I didn't expect to see that, and my anger at seeing it, I didn't expect either.

After that, alone, after a gig, Old Grand Dad[78] and I had a little talk. There's wisdom in age you know. After a little bit a getting' to know each other, I swear that old man said, "Bix robbed you, but not of money." Robbed me of what, then? But Grand Dad didn't say nothing back. Still, I try to honor Bix by imitating the soft tones that came out of his horn. Those tones washed my anger away about being robbed.

CHAPTER 13

LONELINESS GOT THE BEST OF ME

One birthday, maybe it was 1926 or 27, Jimmy Nosek bought me a whore. It all seemed like a big joke at the time. Jimmy did all the negotiating. My knees shook. "Sure is cold," I told Jimmy, just in case he heard my teeth chattering. The Madame, she brings us in the front room, and we buy drinks. I thought the glasses was dirty, and I'm not picky you got to understand. She parades in some of the ladies of the night. Jimmy says of one of them. "Whew, like five miles of bad track!"

The whore, she's got her hands on her hips, snaps back, taking offense, "Hey buddy, you looked in the mirror lately?" I got a laugh out of that 'cause Jimmy thought he was a good-looking guy.

The whole thing the way I remember it was the quiet. The quiet was the foreman that gave the orders. Somehow I got some dame holding me by the arm, and I didn't say nothing. It was quiet enough that I heard myself swallow, and I was thinking at the time if I could take a leak first, I'd feel a lot better. The whore wasn't interested in talking. Whatever was on our minds were our secrets. That was what we had in common. She had a cornflower blue dress on, and someone else came to mind. As much as I tried, she wouldn't look me in eyes. Shoulda walked out, but I didn't because I didn't want to ask myself later what I had missed. So I went through with it like a lotta things in my life.

I follow the whore up the stairs where the rooms were. Those wood stairs creaked, and they seemed to buckle the whore's knees. Some old crow at the top of the stairs says to no one, "Go to room 10," and without lookin' at me, hands me a key in one hand and holds her other one out for a tip.

The whore wore a pretty ribbon that matched her dress. I kept looking at it close up because I didn't want to look at her, and I'm sure she didn't want to look at me. When I pulled down my drawers I was surprised to see I was hard. "What coulda done that?" I said to the quiet in my head. All I remember then was the inside of her thighs felt like chicken from Sterek the butcher. Maybe warmer. I tried to make no noise. Not sure she even breathed. After it, the whore gets dressed in the time it took me to pull my socks back on. As she's walking to the door, I notice because somehow I really didn't before, the whore was a woman. Whore is what she did to get by. She turns and gives me this crooked kind of smile. "So everybody's happy now?"

Gave Jimmy the thumbs up and a big smile when I came back downstairs. His heart was in the right place. Mine wasn't. He slaps me on the back as we walk out, "Happy birthday!" I promised myself when I sat down to write this, I wouldn't hold back nothing.

Don't know about Prague or other cities in Bohemia, but I'll tell you something about Chicago. At night, when you've got the streets to yourself, the loneliness shakes your bones. The streets are wide and empty. The square buildings have edges like knife blades. Downtown is the worst. Flashes of blue electric light from the El[79] is like somebody taking an x-ray of the city. All them windows in the big buildings, but you can't see in. Every sound reminds me of an echo.

One night I'm standing in line to get into the DeLuxe Café[80], and there's this guy standing in front of me raising a storm and making everybody laugh. We get into a little bit of back and forth and joking around. It turns out it's "Mezz" Mezzrow.[81] The guy seating everybody comes outside and says, "Okay, I got a table for four. Any groups of four?" Well Mezz was with two gals, and he looks at me and says, "Hey George join us, and we can make four." So I did. Mezz and I had both come to hear Alberta Hunter.[82] When we learned how much the other cat liked blues and jazz, we hit it off even more. I told him I was a disciple of jazz and he told me, "I'm a damned apostle of jazz, one of the originals through and through. Man, when I play the clarinet I'm the Messiah what came to make crippled men stand up and dance."

Mezz was a Jew, so he told me, but he also said he wanted to be a Negro because only the black man has the true soul for blues and jazz. Said Africa done it, and slavery done it. I don't know about the Africa part, but I do know there's lots of different kinds of slavery besides working in cotton fields. Every kind of slavery makes you look for freedom. Jazz is freedom. And I do know there's no jazz without blues, and there's no blues without the Negro. And in case I doubted that, listening to Alberta Hunter sing her set took all the doubt away. Her body was the music. Her voice was her body. The words of the songs moved.

Of the two ladies, one seemed special to Mezz. My guess is she was part Negro—a handsome woman, slim and affectionate. The other one by the name of Katherine Becker, a red-head born and raised in Wisconsin around Richland Center, I think, eyed Mezz and laughed at all his jokes, but she paid attention to me, too. You'll think I'm a liar, and maybe the shade wasn't quite right, but she was wearing a dress she called robin's egg blue, but it looked the color of a cornflower to me.

Underneath the table, I felt her pretty shoe touch my pant leg. When I moved my leg a little closer to hers, she didn't move away. My breathing came up short. From that moment, everything caught fire. I was as hooked as a fish on a lure. All I wanted was Katherine. I wanted to swallow her whole. If she'd said, "Jump off the Michigan Avenue Bridge." I woulda done it. No shot of junk could possibly equal where this woman took me.

And Katherine, she seemed to double down her interest when she found out I was a jazzman too. She'd hang around the bandstand and wink at me while I soloed. She didn't seem to care how late we played; she'd wait for me and then take care of me the way only a woman can. Time seemed to slow down, and the future was bright. I did some recordings.[83]

Time beat different when I was with Katherine. She held me with a note in her right hand, and the left played a melody. How long does a song last? It can go on in your mind forever. The notes are just as clear. They play back. And something about it makes you not want to let go of the song. Time beat different. And I lost track of the beats one day, but I don't know how many days I had been on the beat when I lost track.

In those days I was getting a lot of work and building a reputation, plus I still had my factory job. Uncle Tomas had taught me well. So I was dressed pretty well, at least not embarrassing. All the Neprases had good straight teeth. "Why not start a band?" I was saying to her, playing too much of the big shot for where I really was, but she encouraged me, blinking her green eyes. You could look into those eyes and read what she was thinking. Uncle Tomas would have been pissed, but I was taking money from the bank where I had been saving for a summer house up in the north woods[84] and spending it on swank dinners with Katherine.

Times with Katherine come back to me like a movie. The streets were wet. The only snow left was in the shadows of houses and trees, and in piles along the Western's big iron fence. The wind came from the south carrying a whiff of the stockyards with it. Jurcik's butcher shop was selling butter pressed in the shape of lambs. The White Sox were already in Sarasota, Florida for spring training. Together, we took the streetcar to Riverview.[85] It seemed nothing was on my mind except to have fun and forget everything else.

I especially liked the Shoot the Chutes ride. They lifted you I don't know how many stories up, then they sent you in this car down a giant ramp into a big pool of water. In the back of my mind I can hear this voice calling out as the car comes to the top, "Keep your hands inside the boat." I remember Katherine squealing in the seat in front of me as we went down the chute, cold water splashing everywhere.

The park had this one thing, too that sticks in my mind. Negroes would sit on this bench behind a screen. You paid money to throw baseballs at a target. The Negroes taunted the thrower, saying things like, "You a mule doctor," and things like that. If you hit the target the bench would give way, and the Negro got dunked in the pool. Something sad about seeing white men lined up, paying money to dunk a Negro. And how did those Negroes feel having to do that to put food on the table?

Katherine knew all the tricks. We were in somebody's apartment left alone for a while. Like it was yesterday, I remember we were standing in the small kitchen of this flat somewhere on the near north side. Katherine looks at me over her shoulder and says, "Georgey, I'm starved. What do they got to eat in this joint?"

All the while I'm thinking, eat? I don't want to eat. I want to rip the dress off of her. I have to admit, just to be honest. Unlike Ma in front of the stove heating sauerkraut and sausage, Katherine pulls a chair over to the stove and puts her foot up on the chair. She's wearing these pretty patent leather shoes with bows that drove me crazy. Katherine pulls back her skirt so she can adjust her black silk stocking.

"Georgey," she says, "I'm cooking some nice stuff tonight."

Sometimes I can be real dumb. "Cooking nice stuffing? What stuffing? I don't smell nothing cookin.'"

"You don't," and she gives me this look, "It's about ready to boil over."

I peek over at the stove.

"You're a big shot musician right?"

"You bet," I says back.

"Then come here, big shot musician. Play me a love song."

"My cornet's on the sofa."

"Forget blowin' in that cornet of yours, hot lips."

It comes to me what she's after. So I kind of sashay over to her.

"Help me fix my stocking," she says real smooth like.

I go up to her and blow in her ear like it was the mouthpiece of my cornet. She scrunches her neck and giggles. Then she turns her head and licks my neck and wraps that leg that's up on the chair around my thighs. That silk stocking's got me wrapped tight. Thought my pants would blow open. Oh baby, we jammed a duet till the sun come up.

One night we're walking along the sidewalk after a gig. What do you think I learn from her? Turns out her mother is a Bohemian! By the name of Bezdek. The story she told me was the factory workers went to Chicago and the farmers to Wisconsin and Nebraska.[86] You never stop learning. How could I go wrong, the gal was a Bohunk? And she knew how to make Knedliki.

In the midst of all this, I come home one morning. I had to get ready for work. 'Cause I was still a young guy, I was burning the candle at both ends and getting by. Suppose now, years later, I have to admit, I was gone more than I was there. Wasn't paying attention to anything but me and Katherine and my music. Exactly, I can't even honestly say how long I'd been like that other than to say by then my eyes were bloodshot and my belly shrank. Didn't have time on Saturdays to pick up kolaczky or nothing. Well, as soon as I cracked the door to the kitchen, I knew something wasn't right. Something stunk awful. Then I seen it. Ma was on the kitchen floor. Only knew it was Ma for sure by the dress I recognized. Dead don't describe what I saw.

They took her away and called it natural causes. It was like one of them nightmares where you can't get someplace you're supposed to be. I wasn't where I was supposed to be when the gal I loved died, and I wasn't with my own Ma when she passed. You're not supposed to neglect your family. Where the hell had I been? Hadn't gotten sacked at work and hadn't missed playing a tune, but I wasn't even sure the month or the day. Creepin' around in the back of my head was the thought that Katherine had been slippin' something in my drinks. How else do you explain leaving your Ma one day and finding her half decomposed and you think maybe a night but not more than two has passed?

The next door neighbors, the Czernys, told the police I had murdered Ma. The "Dick" investigating, just shook his head. He was a nice guy and said, "Look pal, I know you didn't do it, but because you been accused, I got to ask some questions." For two hours he asked me mostly the same things over and over again. Katherine backed me up, but she wasn't about to help clean up, and she didn't like hanging around the house. The neighbors took her for a gold-digger on account of the fashionable things she wore. I don't blame her for not wanting to be around. To this day, on a rainy damp day in early spring or the fall, I swear I can still smell Ma.

The wake and funeral was closed casket. Ma was always complaining that she didn't want to get planted at The Bohemian National Cemetery because it was filled with "them scum free-thinkers." Guess she put Pa in that category best I can remember. She claimed to be a good Catholic and hung a rosary on the bedroom door. The way it banged back and forth when you moved the door drove Pa crazy. But what was I gonna do? There was a paid for plot at Bohemian National, so it's where I buried her.

Then I sat thinking. My thinking was someplace behind my life. Things needed catching up. There was Katherine babying me. Making me feel good. But she was also getting pouty when I didn't want to go out. Eventually, she said she could do something with the house. She had real strong opinions about the kitchen. It wasn't a kitchen like you saw in magazines. But nobody was touching the house and especially the kitchen. Katherine cooked some swell meals for me, and she made a pie once but the crust wasn't just right. My walks bothered her. I was too fast for her dainty shoes.

So then one evening she's over at the house, and Katherine started saying that she hated my factory job. She scratched at everything about me. "It's a loser's job," she kept saying and that made me go real quiet. I tried to tell her about Uncle Tomas and his place in the North Woods.

She said, "Big deal!"

"What do you want anyway?" I'd ask.

"More than this." But she tried to be encouraging too. Said I could be more. I could be famous. Said she had faith in me.

A cymbal banged in my head; hey, forty wasn't that far off[87] and let's face it, a lot of times things just don't pan out. Katherine wanted everything to turn out the way she planned them. That don't work. I tried to tell her that sometimes you don't have to run your head up against the wall. You can walk around it. Maybe she was that way 'cause she was so young and pretty.

One day I'm thinking about jazz, and I didn't notice her dress, so she says, "You only think about yourself."

"What?" I says back.

"You only worry about what makes you happy."

"That ain't true," I answer back getting' kinda huffy.

"There you go lying to me."

"Don't call me no liar."

"You're a liar!"

I was always straight with her. And I wasn't only thinking about me. So I says, "I ain't selfish!"

"Prove it."

"I'll do anything for you," I says. "I'd follow you anywhere."

She says back, "Give me that cornet of yours!"

"Katherine, I can't give you that."

"See! Liar, liar!" With that she shuts herself in the bedroom.

But I figure, it's best to be calm. So I go to the door and turn the knob, the one with the rosary hanging on it. Son of a bitch it's locked. "What's gotten into you, Katherine," I'm shouting now. Imagine that. In my Ma's room!

From inside I hear her screaming, "You're crude; you're crude," or some such shit as that. "You're just like all the Bohunks. I was warned. They never treat a lady nice."

So I scream through the door so she can hear it, "What the hell you talkin' about. I spend half my day doing stuff for you."

"Liar, liar!"

"Don't say that." Why was she doing this?

"Leave me alone you rough man!"

So I told her, "Get the hell outta Ma's room."

So what does she tell me, she tells me, "Don't threaten me!"

That did it see? I don't threaten ladies. I kicked the door, and heard it crack open.

Katherine lets out a scream that'd either kill you or bring you back to life. She's holding her hands in front of her face like I'm gonna belt her or something. Next thing you know, I got her by the dress and I'm saying, "But Katherine I love you. Can't you get that through your thick noggin'?"

And what do I get for that? She's trying to kick me in the balls and scratch me in the eye. That's when the knocks on the front door start. It was the cops. Both of us freeze. Never seen a change come over anyone so fast in all my life. She's straightening her dress, her hair. As calm as she can be, she's putting on fresh lipstick. The smile on her face was as sweet as when I saw her at the club the first time with Mezz.

She sweet-talked the cops right out of there. They tipped their hats on the way out. What the hell was this woman, I'm thinking. For a good fifteen minutes after they left, I was still standing there at the door, staring out to nowhere, and in the background, I hear Katherine humming some happy tune I couldn't quite catch, but I knew it, I know I'd heard it before. All I could think was the pieces didn't fit no more, like a screwed up musical arrangement.

What happened after that causes my heart to ache from guilt more than anything else. At the time I blamed it on Katherine coming on too strong. Oh, I didn't do nothing to stop her. Still, Stella was my gal. I'm not a total fool. I know Stella was long gone. Katherine and I was quite a couple for a handful of hot months. Ever hear Louis Armstrong sing, *It Was Just One of Those Things*?[88]

> "*If we had thought a bit of the end of it*
> *When we started painting the town*
> *We'd been aware that our love affair*
> *Was too hot not to cool down*
> *A trip to the moon duh dee dee duh bob or however it goes*
> *It was just one of those things.*"

Then she started crying all the time and hanging on to my coat when it was clear I wasn't paying her no mind. It was a torture because how could I be what she wanted? The closer she tried to be, the more alone I felt. Her tears felt like ice water, and her pouting lips were a piano out of tune. For all of her kindnesses she didn't understand how mixed up I was after Ma passed. She found out ways to punish me, to make me feel small like when I was practicing my cornet, and she held her hands over her ears. One night she didn't show up at the gig where I was playing.

That's when I made a decision. I needed to get out of Chicago. A band down in St. Louis had asked me to join them. Bix had been down there. If it was good enough for him, it was good enough for me. They needed a cornet, and they played the old style hot music. I needed jazz, not pouting Katherine. "Hello Central give me Doctor Jazz. he's got what I need. I say he has."[89] And so one morning I told 'em at work I was through. I shut off the lights in the house, paid the bills. locked the doors and took the job. And I didn't even tell Katherine. Didn't write; didn't visit; didn't try to make a telephone call; didn't try to leave a message with her friends at the cleaners where she worked. Sometimes you know when you are going to regret something and sometimes you don't.

All I took was one suitcase and my horn. To this day I can feel that morning at the Illinois Central Station climbing on board that Gulf Mobile and Ohio maroon colored train. The morning was cold and rainy, and there was a fog out on Lake Michigan. I half expected to see Katherine running down the platform to try to stop me, but she didn't know I was there. Nobody did. Not Zeke or Jimmy Nosek. Maybe Stella did. When the door closed and the train started to chug away, I almost jumped off. Something about it was like when Bix went away. I thought I was doing the right thing, but it didn't feel right in my heart. The whole world didn't like the day either. The papers called it "Black Tuesday."[90] That's all anybody talked about on the train. Me leaving Katherine like that. That was black enough.

There's about nothing lonelier than crossing the flat farmland of Illinois when the crops are in, but nothing's sprouted, and the ground is barren with the sky so gray, it takes the horizon away, and you can see your breath, but it ain't that cold. Little drops of rain dribbled along the dirty train window. And then there's the train whistle, *whoo-whoo-eee*.

Finally, we chugged over the Mississippi, brown and swollen, churning and rolling. I knew the piece I was looking at had already passed where Bix was born, and it was heading down past Algiers where jazz was born. And I was somehow hoping to be reborn and for a minute or two as we were crossing the bridge, I wanted to jump in and get bathed in it. I look at that water, and I feel real affection. That river and saying its name brings tears to my eyes. "It goes to my head and lingers like a haunting refrain."[91]

My time in St. Louis was a blur. I found some rooming house on Olive near Lindell. Often it was a comfort to stop in the big gray church there at Saint Louis University. I'd listen to the Mass early in the morning after I'd played the night away. Tears would come to my eyes when the altar boy rang the bell and the priest raised the host over his head. For so much I wanted to be forgiven, but when it came to stepping in the confessional I didn't know what to say. Sometimes I'd get a hot dog and a root beer at Garavelli's Café. They had this good toasted ravioli too. Garavelli's had this mezzanine, and I sat up there and watched the people. I should have written down the songs that came to me. If the colored were treated bad in Chicago, it was worse there. A gloom hung over that city. And I made sure my door was locked and a chair propped up under the knob every night.

The band didn't last. The clubs were closing down. I got work where I could. My pants got a shine to them. I even played on street corners, but the cops don't like that. Finally, knowing the bankroll was about run out, I took a powder and headed back to Chicago, back over the same bridge but at least the corn was up, green and knee-high when we crossed the fields.

Chapter 14

The Coming of Swing

It don't mean a thing if ain't got that swing.[92] There was less syncopation and more arrangements, and it was damn harder to find work even back in Chicago with the Depression and all. The jazz scene was New York now. Bix had been right. It had been heading that way. First it was the Illinois Central carrying the New Orleans jazzmen north to Chicago, and now it was the New York Central taking them to New York. I was back in the house. One neighbor said, "What the hell are you doing back? I thought you were dead."

And I says back, "I came back from the dead to finish my work here on earth, just as I promised, see."

"Big deal!" I remember him saying.

My words sounded brave, but I figure I was getting only a third the work I had before I left for St. Louis. And I didn't have the factory job.

I hung around Zeke's a lot sipping cups of joe. Zeke hadn't changed. You could tell him anything. He'd heard it all more than once. When I came in the first time after St. Louis he asked, "Where you been Pal?" So I told him the whole story about St. Louis and how I walked out on Katherine.

He pushed his paper hat back on his head and whistled, "Whew, St. Valentine's Day Massacre."[93] he said that in his dry hoarse voice.

Zeke was skinnier than the day I met him. Maybe it had something to do with getting gassed[94] in the war. Every once in a while, when Zeke turned his head, you got a glimpse of those mustard gas scars, the flesh was all twisted and red. Once, Zeke told me what happened. He was running across the battlefield and jumped in a shell hole. The mustard gas had mixed in the water at the bottom of the hole. Zeke told me they played a brass band for him when he shipped off to France, and when he got back after the war, they "sent his ass to a hospital that might as well have been the Cook County jail." Now, nobody talked about the Great War. I guess it wasn't so great no more. There were enough problems without worrying about the old ones.

Finally, I found some day work sweeping out the grandstands at Hawthorne Park Race Track.[95] As I swept I whistled *Stella by Starlight*. All them tickets, somebody hoping to score big. Piles of tickets and cigarette butts. It's like the sky snowed them into the stands. Every one of those tickets I swept up was a loser: number 9 to show in the seventh, number six to place in the third, and the crazy new thing, the daily double. With what did they buy these tickets— the dinner money, milk money for the kids—hell I don't know. Lots of people were doing okay in the Depression. Maybe these people had the money to burn.

If I had all the money these people lost, I'd be a swell with a big car. Wouldn't that surprise them two next door? I'd pull up in a big Packard. There they are! I can see them, the brother and sister lookin' out the front room window with their heads together like two cheeks on a fat ass. But I really didn't want that kind of fast money then, and I don't want it now. I want something that puts you in tune. Something that allows you to go to bed at night and let your eyes close grateful you had the chance to make something that reached out beyond yourself.

What I wanted I found in an old metal shed near the rail yard. I'd go there at night and bring my horn. I'd practice, and then I'd practice some more. I was in a place where nobody could see me, and I couldn't see them. All there was, was what I created and I gave it to that dirty rail yard for free. The train whistles blew, and I blew back at them. And I felt close to things, and life didn't seem so complicated. My jazz in that shed was pure and sweet.

In 1933 the World's Fair came to Chicago. It was called "The Century of Progress."[96] It gave me some breathing space because a good jazzman could find all the work he needed. Millions and millions of people visited that fair. It was the most important thing in the world. It showed you what the future would look like with all them scientific inventions. But the future didn't turn out exactly the way they had it laid out. Just like WWI wasn't "the war to end all wars."[97]

I saved an entrance ticket. Somebody told me it would be worth plenty someday. I keep it in Pa's old lunch pail with that bottle of valve oil Bix gave me. Some other things are in there too. There's a holy card with a picture of St. Adalbert, the patron saint of Prague. The prayer's in Bohemian, so I can't read it. Ma had brought it with her on the ship across the ocean. Then there's this picture, a real old picture, of Ma and Pa down in the old Pilsen neighborhood. A postcard with a picture of the castle in Krumlov is in there. Pa's union card is precious, and it's in there. He believed in workers' rights even if he did come to Chicago to break strikes. Shows a man can change a point of view. Of course, the thing in that pail that's most precious to me is the ticket to the Sokol hall to see Stella play. I can still feel the warmth of her pretty hand on that ticket when she handed it to me at Kryl's apartment.

As hard as times were, I made an investment decision. I took a bundle of cash I saved up from my jobs and bought a trumpet I found cheap in a pawnshop. The way jazz was going, you had to have a trumpet. The cornet was too harsh. A trumpet with a mute on it had that right swing sound. It took the staccato away and made the sound dreamier. People needed to fill their bellies with something when you wonder when you're getting' your next loaf of bread. Some evenings when I didn't have a gig I polished up my old silver Conn and my new trumpet, and I heard the jazz in my mind, and the faces on the people were happy. Sometimes I just sat back and looked at those two shiny horns and took soft deep breaths. In those times, I confess, I cried from being thankful for being invited into the life I had.

It was about this time I remember walking through the neighborhood after I had gotten done with a gig. It was a warm evening and still early by my standards, too early for bed. The wind was blowing the bacon smell of the chemical plant over in Stickney through the neighborhood. Then again maybe the smell was coming from the stink of Al Capone and his thugs.[98] I walked over to the school. The sign still hung on the back wall, "No hardball playing allowed."

I cupped my hands over my eyes and peeked through the window of my old eighth-grade classroom. Seemed like the same desks were bolted to the floor. I half expected to see Miss Stepanek standing in front of the classroom. I said to myself, I can't remember one thing I learned in that room, but I remember Miss Stepanek, and the break she gave me. A sadness played blues notes through me. I wished she was there to thank her again. She probably never knew as the years went on how much happiness she had given me by letting my life swing to music.

Something had changed in my life. Maybe it was that I was in my thirties. It was like the warehouse near the rail yard. It was empty now. The year before, the cops had found a still in it. The prairie was trying to take it back. Goldenrod grew where the trucks used to park. At a distance nothing looked different, but something, somewhere had left, packed up and left. Something had emptied out.

That night I spent four hours washing the dirty dishes that was stacked in the sink. Cleaned the stove and scrubbed the floor even on the spot where Ma had been. I saw the kitchen needed new tiles. I remembered Pa laying that floor, screaming "shit" when something didn't go right, and I remember Ma screaming about his screaming.

On the next Friday night I played in a swing band that claimed to be the "the best around with the New York sound." Thank God Kryl had taught me to read music, because with swing everything was written out and arranged. A lot of the best jazzmen got shoved right off the train and left to die because they couldn't read music. Good men who knew their horns better than their lungs that powered them. Some of them went back home to the south. Some got themselves lost on booze. Some who gave starts to some of the big names, and I'm not gonna name any names here, never got help. I never could understand how you could ignore somebody who helped you. Instead, they walked right over their backs. I seen it. Many a time I bought a cup of joe and a slice of apple pie for those old musicians. I'd let them go on talkin' about their lives, and I let them know they were great men. Too many times, they were the Negro men who had come north up the Mississippi with the hot music. I spared them a dime[99] when I could. But it was tough to look a man in the eyes who had so much hopelessness. They looked like I imagine those poor folks drowning on the Eastland must have looked, like poor Stella's father. Sometimes life just runs out of options and the song don't pan out the way you planned.

All the men in the swing band wore tuxedoes, and we had a red-headed singer who wore one of them elegant gowns. She was pretty when she was all dolled up. It was a big band: three clarinets, two trombones, drums, a bass, three trumpets, a couple of saxophones, and a piano. We jazzed up the solos, but even the solos were written out, and we knew who was going to play next. In the twenties it was more of a competition. That's part of why the music was so hot. You got a solo by challenging the guy playing. You had to be quick and right on the music, ready to do musical gymnastics by that I mean syncopating.

I liked the swing sound, but it didn't have any craziness. Now I know a lot jazz fans out there are going to say, "Whataya mean, you tellin' me Count Basie[100] didn't have craziness?" Well, I have to admit that his song, *One O'clock Jump*, has got plenty of everything. But to me, and I got a right as an American citizen to say it, swing didn't have no factory sounds, no rail yards, no late night streets with lonely people, no sitting in the bright light of Zeke's place with the night trying to creep its way inside. It was sentimental and made you want to fall in love or dance. Besides, just then, it was the only jazz in town. Swing had taken roots like the goldenrod around the warehouse. So I figured the best thing to do was be a part of it. What other choice did I have? It wasn't the first tough decision I'd faced being a syncopator. If this was the only jazz in town, then I needed to be a part of it. It is important in life to have something you will stick with. Something you can say after the last set you play in life, "I never gave up."

In the end, the band didn't last. We kept playing in worse and worse joints. One night we were playing in Gary, Indiana. It wasn't the Pump Room in the Palmer House[101] if you know what I mean. It's only your faith in God sometimes that keeps you from trembling, and in Gary back then, you had to ask yourself if God was real. Belching factories, dirty politics, crime, wasted people, folks burning themselves out on pleasure of the moment. Even the sky seemed to be burning from the blast furnaces there. The joint we played in had colored strips of paper hanging from the ceiling that made the whole place even sadder. The place was packed with shills and punks looking to make trouble. Somehow it was connected to a parish. Maybe they did it to beef up their confession business because you could feel the joint ready to explode into a brawl.

I finished a solo and looked out at the dance crowd. I saw the blue dress before I saw her face. It was Katherine. She was looking right at me, and the look she gave me was so sad. It tugged my heart. I remember once Tommy Dorsey[102] tells me back when he was playing with Bix, "It's like musicians were made to make dames break their hearts."

Instantly, I knew what to do. I'd been carrying the guilt and shame of walking out on Katherine too long. The second the song was over, I jumped down off the stage and walked right up to her.

Even before I could open my mouth she says, "George, why did you walk out on me? I waited so long George…" Her eyes filled with tears.

"Katherine, I don't know…" It was all I could think to say. I don't know to this day why I was so cruel.

The tears ran down her cheeks. "You should never have come back now. George, you're mean to show me your face again."

The bandleader's behind me, "Hey George, we got music to play, get back on the stage."

"Right," I says to him, and then I turn to Katherine, "Wait for me. Wait for me. I got things I gotta tell you."

She was bawling by then, and I see her head shaking no. "Just wait till this set is over."

I run back to the stage, and when I climb back on and get in my seat, I stare out to the crowd, but I don't see her nowhere. And then, we're into another song. All I can do is turn to my music. It seemed like hours before the break came after our set. I looked all over the joint. Asked the bouncers. They wouldn't give me the time of day let alone tell me whether they saw Katherine leave. Seeing her made the hurt even worse, and by the look of Katherine's face, if anything, she was even worse off. That night I resolved to find Katherine, so I could square things with her.

Sometimes we are all so hopeless. We concentrate on what isn't important, and we push people aside. Oh, we all have reasons for what we do, selfish reasons. Once I remember running into a dame who Jimmy left in a bad way. I don't even remember her last name. It was late. A street lamp's light cut through the cold foggy air like a minor note on a sax. As I buttoned up my collar I seen her.

"Missed my streetcar," she says.

"Looks like you and me are gonna catch the last run."

"Got going the wrong way on one car, so I'm starting over."

"Yep, done that plenty of times."

She kinda smiled, "So I'm not the only dummy around here?"

"Naw."

"I didn't mean nothing bad by that."

"Oh hell, I know that." I don't know what got into me. I says, "I'm sorry about you and Jimmy breakin' up."

She had a hard time holding in the tears when the streetcar comes. I sit next to her. She was dabbing her eyes with a hankie. I said to her. "I'll ride with you to your stop. A lady shouldn't be out alone."

She thanks me. Then we don't talk. She just stares out the window, but I could see her reflection in the glass. I guess you could say that her time had passed by, but she had a sincere face, an honest face that made me want to protect her. I hope someone is there to protect Katherine. And I hope someone—Stella's father, or some stranger even—in that dark cold water when the Eastland turned over, held Stella and let her know she wasn't alone.

Finally, this lady, and I don't remember her name, says, "Well, this is my stop."

I say to her, "Okay, but I can't just leave you feeling like this. Let me buy you a bite to eat."

"That's nice, but I couldn't ask you..."

We're already moving to the front of the car. "Forget about it. Come on, I'm hungry."

"Well maybe a cup of coffee."

"Sure, whatever."

We found this all night joint. A typical Chicago place, DeMars, LeMar's, something like that. You know, it was a fountain specialties kinda place, steaks, chops, breakfast anytime, with booths and a counter. It was the kind of place where you could always pick up the first edition of the paper. Jazz hid in every corner of the place. I talked her into pancakes to go with her joe. When we got inside, we both shook off the outside chill.

We didn't talk much. I recall how she cut neat triangles out of her stack of hotcakes. She didn't just pour syrup all over them like I do. No, she poured just a little bit at a time, real dainty and ladylike.

She had a face on her that reminded me of the way a boy looks who's been picked last for a sandlot baseball game. Finally I says, "I'm sorry it's not going the way you want."

She shrugs her shoulders. She was still wearing her coat, and it had some kind of fur collar, but the coat was too big for her. I can remember that. Isn't that something? And other things I can't remember at all. "Yeah, I guess it's a mess," she says.

And we let it alone and left things unsaid. I was so angry at Jimmy. Then she says, "Thanks for the pancakes and coffee. I better get on home." Her eyes were off somewhere else. A couple of tears go rolling down her cheek and smudges her eye make-up. "I think I did bad things."

I took a paper napkin and dipped it in my glass of water and reached over and cleaned the smudge away. "You're okay now."

I think I heard her say 'cause she was whispering it almost. "You're a peach."

"Sure, sure, don't let me hold you up." We stand up. I was going to offer to walk her to her door, but then I thought the better of it. She wanted to be by herself. I don't think another word was spoke between us.

I didn't have money to hire a private dick or nothing to find Katherine. Had to do it on my own. I remembered Katherine had an aunt by the same last name living down in Pullman.[103] I think she called her Aunt Polly. So one day I take myself down to Pullman and that ain't no easy trip from Cicero. Pullman was like a different world, but I dug up the address pretty easily. Got directions from some grouchy neighbors, but they didn't steer me wrong.

When I get to the address, there's this green Plymouth coupe parked in front of the house. Some guy with a slick double-breasted suit was walking out the front door. He had a toothpick and butt jammed in his mouth like the mobsters. The shoulders on this guy made him look like a brick shithouse. He climbs in the car, slamming the door behind him, guns the engine, and peels about an inch of rubber off his tires as he squealed off.

Some old lady, wearing a red dress that was probably already too tight a couple of years before, is standing in the doorway with her arms folded in front of her. She's giving an evil stare to that car that peeled off. She's got a pack of Pall Malls in one hand, and she's jamming a lit butt between lips painted with the brightest lipstick I ever seen. "Aunt Polly?"

"Who's asking Bub? You some kind of cop?"

"No. I'm George Nepras."

"Then what are you selling 'cause I ain't buyin.'"

I see a shadow cross behind her. Something about the shadow makes me think it's Katherine. In the corner of my right eye, I see the curtains in the front window move a little bit. "I'm not trying to sell you nothing lady."

"Then why don't you scram?" I think I remember her asking.

"Hey, I'm trying to see if Katherine Becker's here. I want to talk that's all."

She kinda gives me this half smile and blows out this big cloud of smoke, "Even the talk's not free here."

"I came all the way from Cicero."

Cicero seemed to grab her attention. "Cicero? You connected?"

"To what?" I ask, "You gonna help me or what?"

For a second I get an itch like she's gonna let me in. Her face had that, "what the hell, why not, no sweat off my back" look. Then she turns her head and looks back inside. When she looks back she searches the street up and down. Some car on the other side of the street catches her attention, so she's not lookin' at me when she says, "Naw. Why don't you scram? No Katherine here." With that she turns around and walks inside and slams the door. I hear the lock being thrown.

"Hey!" I shout, and I pound a couple of times on the door.

That's when I notice two guys get out of the car across the street and start walking my way. They climb the steps. I make 'em to be flatfoots. One says to me, "Beat it." The other one gives me the head jerk and says, "Do yourself a favor. Do what my partner asked."

"Okay, okay," I says. If I knew for sure Katherine had been inside I might of tried some heroics, but sometimes you have to let things go. On the long ride back to Cicero, I didn't think about Katherine once, and I never felt guilty after that. Sometimes you know when you have to leave it go.

One day I'm perusin' the paper at Zeke's when I come across this ad. Benny Goodman[104] is coming back to Chicago from New York to play the swankiest places. He was holding auditions. I ripped that ad out of the paper and went home to practice.

When I walked into that hotel ballroom to take a crack at it, I was feeling pretty good. There Benny was up front, hair a little thinner and a few more pounds, but I recognized the cat. As soon as he takes a look at me he says, "Don't I know you from someplace?"

"Sure," I says back. "We used to listen together at the clubs in the old days. Listened together to Johnny Dodds[105] play the licorice stick once."

A smile came over his face. "That's it. Wow, Johnny Dodds! There was a great one. I could never get enough of him."

What a gentleman Benny was. Some say he was cold, all business, rough on his musicians. He was an important jazzman, and I'll tell you, he treated me square. We chatted like we was both living back in Chicago. Says to me, "So you're one of the old Chicago gang?"

"We practically grew up in the same neighborhood, you and me."

"You lived near Maxwell Street?"

"Used to shop there all the time with my Ma. Started out in Pilsen, then we moved to Cicero."

"Sure, Pilsen was close. So you're a Bohemian kid." Pokes himself in the chest. "Poland and Russia for me. Maxwell Street. Those were the days."

"That's when a buck meant something."

Benny, he smiles. "What are you going to play for us, George?"

I played some Jelly Roll Morton stuff. Took a chance that the old hot jazz would connect with him. No doubt about it, I played my heart out, and when I was through, Benny applauded. And he stopped the auditions, to personally walk me to the back of the theater. "You were good, George, you were real good," he says, and he's holding my elbow in a kind way. "I don't think I can use you this time around, George, I'm looking for a special kind of sound for this gig."

"I understand," I says back. "Don't think nothing of it." Later, when I thought about it, I didn't understand too well.

"You keep in touch. If you get out to New York, you look me up. You play a mean horn." Benny Goodman was a gentleman. A jazzman has to learn to suck it up.

CHAPTER 15

Stormy Weather

I can hear Lena Horne singing it on the record, "Don't know why, there's no sun up in the sky, stormy weather.... it's raining all the time."[106]

Maybe a few days later, I'm not exactly sure, I stop into Zeke's 'cause that was my custom, but Zeke wasn't there. Some other guy that don't look like Zeke at all is standing behind the counter with the same white hat and white apron. "Can I help you? Want something to eat?"

I guess I was standing there staring. "Where's Zeke?"

"The guy that runs the joint?"

"Yeah."

"They told me they brought him to the hospital."

"Hospital, what hospital?"

"Calm down neighbor. How the hell should I know?"

"Didn't they tell ya?"

"They didn't tell me hardly nothing. Told me start work on Monday, brother, and here I am. In the position I'm in I don't ask no questions." The guy starts scratching the back of his head, thinking about it like, trying to be helpful, and the white paper hat tips down over his forehead practically covering one of his eyes. "Wait," and he sticks his finger out like he caught something on it. "I heard the veterans' hospital."

I was out of there before the guy could say another word. First thing I did was go to Jana's bakery. Nothing like bringing bakery when somebody's sick. I bought a dozen kolaczky. Irene waited on me as usual. Irene was one of my favorites. Had these big thick glasses, always smiling; don't think I ever saw her in a bad mood.

"You are lookin' nice today, Irene."

"George, there you go with the flattery."

"Well see, you get better and better. It's in that good Bohemian baking."

She waved her hand at me. "Don't be a silly goose."

I rested my arms on the counter above the salty horns and kaiser rolls. It smelled of yeast and caraway seed, and sweetness. My God I had been buying bakery there since we moved to Cicero. "So how's "Matka? (mother)"

"Ah George, I'll tell ya," she says, "It's no good getting' old." She had this habit of flipping her hand up like she was tossing something away. "Ninety-one she is. Every day I make her a nice polevaka. I strain the vegetables, see. No seeds or nothing, mostly just the juice from the cooked meat, no pieces."

"Soup's best they say. You're a good daughter Irene."

"What choice do I have, she's my mother."

"You're doing the right thing. Hey, when I'm through here, I'm going right to the parish. Gonna light a couple of candles. Can't hurt, right?"

"Oh, George thank you." I remember seeing a little tear. "Enjoy yourself, it's later than you think." With that she sticks a custard bismarck in a bag and whispers, emphasizing each word with her lips, "A little treat for you when you get home."

Finally, we get down to business. "So what'll it be today?"

"A dozen mixed kolaczky."

Irene clasps her cheeks with her hands. "You gonna eat all them, George?"

"Hey I'm a growing boy."

Irene waves her hand at me. "Yeah sure."

"They're for a sick friend, Irene."

"Oh, then God bless," and she makes the sign of the cross. "You said you want me to mix 'em up?"

"Tell you what, Irene," I says back, "Give me three cheese, three svestkova povidla (prune jam), three merunky (apricot), and three Mak (poppy seed paste)."

"You got it." They go into the white box that she ties with the string that comes off the big roll near the cash register. After I pay, Irene hands me the box and says, "You tell your friend I'll keep him in my prayers."

I says back, "Irene, we keep talking, and we'll be praying for everybody in Chicago."

"And Bohemia."

The bell over the door jingled. A new customer came in, and we stopped talkin'.

Well, I found the hospital. A helluva big place. Get greeted on Zeke's floor by some kind of nurse blocking my way with an enamel bedpan full of piss. The floor smelled sharp with medicine and sweet rot like a bad can of bully beef I opened once. The meat was black, and it took two days to air out the kitchen. Dinging bells, hacking phlegm coughs, and people going this way and that, making the wood floor creak.

Zeke wasn't exactly in a room. The long hallway that vanished off to nowhere someplace ahead, had open areas on both sides. In each open area was four beds and a few chairs. They had windows on one side. The first thing I noticed in Zeke's part was a guy propped up in a wheelchair like he was a washboard. He had no arms or legs, didn't seem to have no ass either. He smiled at me, but I didn't smile back, and I regret that to this day, but see, I wasn't expecting that. I wasn't prepared for it.

Heard someone whisper, "George, George, over here!" It was Zeke calling me from his bed. He looked sucked dry. Maybe it was that Zeke was without his big white apron, Zeke without his white soda jerk hat that he wore like an overseas cap, wasn't Zeke. The guy in the wheelchair and another guy in the room stared at me but didn't say nothing.

"How'd you find me?"

"Ah, it wasn't hard." But I fibbed. Asking for a gas victim on that floor was like asking if a tobacco shop had cigars.

Zeke speaks up some, but you could tell it strained him. "Meet my bunkmates."

I looked around at these old doughboys.[107] The guy in the wheelchair is still smiling at me. I know it sounds crazy, but I swear he looked happy. Another guy was as yellow at the piss in that enamel pot. Zeke saw me looking at the one empty bed.

"They took ol' Bobby out this morning, right boys?"

The other two laughed. I wanted to ask what was so funny, but it was funny to them, and I left it to be their private joke.

"Yeah the guy in the wheelchair says, "Every morning they wheel them from over here to over there."

They all start laughing, and the yellow guy starts singing, *Over There*.[108]

Zeke cuts in, "George here is a famous jazz cornet player and my best customer."

"Nah. Come on Zeke, don't bullshit your buddies," I says back, but I can't deny it felt good for someone to say something nice about me.

"It's true. What you got there?"

"No big deal. Just a dozen kolaczky. Didn't know which kind you liked, so I brought a mix: three prune, three apricot, three cheese, three poppy seed."

"That was swell of you to bring me something." He waves me closer and whispers soft, "Hey George, will you do me a favor?"

"Sure Zeke," I says.

"Would you pass the box around and let my bunkmates have a crack at 'em?"

I put a prune and an apricot one on a plate next to the yellow guy. Up close I could hear he was gurgling a little when he breathed. He says to me his family was Polish, and his mother made "cakes just like these."

Then I came up to the wheelchair. I opened the box. He spoke. "I never seen nothing like these. How about picking for me?"

I hear Zeke say, "Eat one of them, and your life's gonna start all over."

"That good?"

"That good."

I took one of the round, flat cheese kolaczky out of the box, and the wheelchair guy opens his mouth, and I put the whole thing in there on his tongue. He starts chewing real solemn like.

Zeke asks him, "Good right?"

The guy slowly shakes his head yes, and I'll be damned if I didn't see a tear run down his face. Didn't really think kolaczky was that good.

I go over to Zeke's bed. "When you getting sprung from this place?"

"It's not good, George. The gas you know."

"I seen the scars."

"But them's from mustard gas. You can't see the real problem. It's that phosgene gas[109] the Huns got me with."

I told him I'd never heard of no phosgene gas.

"It ripped my lungs up pretty good."

I could tell he had the blues bad. "Come on Zeke." I put my right hand, the one that holds my cornet, on his shoulder."

He whispers, and I can remember like it was two measures of music ago, "I ain't gonna make it. Better I'd died in France. George, pal, I feel so alone. This place. Damn it all to hell. I tried to do the right thing, George, but I got no woman. Not many'll take somebody with mustard gas scars."

I says back to him. "You always did the right thing buddy. I'll stick with ya Zeke."

"Would ya, George? The Heinies didn't scare me, but this, I don't understand what's going on."

"I'll be back tomorrow, it's Thursday. I play a club tonight, but Thursday's open. We'll play cards or something."

"That'd be swell, George."

Zeke didn't make Thursday.

After a while, I sucked it up the best I could and came back to visit Zeke's bunkmates. The yellow guy went next. He smiled on the way out, and the guy in the wheelchair cried and had no hand to wipe the tears away, so I helped, and I held a handkerchief to his nose to blow. We got real close. I stood by him too. I know I've said before that I was going to shoot straight and not hold back nothing. I said I'd tell everything square. But see, this guy told me a lot of stuff in confidence. He counted on me to keep my mouth shut. It seems to me, even though he's gone now, he deserves me respecting that. So a lot of things that were said between us that have made me understand him and have made me a better man and a better syncopator, I'm not going to put in this book. If I can't be a man that can be trusted, then what the hell kind of jazzman am I anyway?

See all you jazz musicians out there, life is hard to figure. That's why you got to hold on to your jazz soul. Everything else passes. Hell, even Prohibition was over in '35, and I figured that was never gonna end.[110] Life can turn on a dime, so you can't give up. Couldn't have been two months after Zeke passed on—his body and not my memory of him—that I got in one of the best swing bands in Chicago. See what I mean? It was a sweet gig. Went non-stop for nine months or more. I was treated well. Stayed in class hotels and met interesting cats. Ate steak smothered in onions whenever I wanted. Brought my trumpet playing up a notch. I was hearing the music inside me day in and day out. That same voodoo followed me about.[111] I started to notice that the name Conn was beginning to be erased by polishing my cornet. How much music had come out of the bell of that horn? Where does the music go? Does it really disappear?

Chapter 16

Darn that Dream[112]

The next summer during one of those humid hot spells that Chicago gets that makes you wonder if snow in Chicago was only a dream and not something that really happened, I got word that Uncle Tomas died. He was bass fishing on a north woods lake near where Tomas's cabin was. It was the first full summer of his retirement. Let's say Uncle Tomas needed a big belt to get around his trousers. He stood up to cast, they say, and the boat tipped and dropped him in five feet of water. Tomas couldn't swim, no place to learn that in the neighborhood. So he panicked, I hear, got all tangled up in the waterweeds and drowned. Aunt Estelle stuffed her head in the cabin gas stove when she heard the news and died too. I got the inheritance, but it wasn't as much as I thought. Seems Uncle Tomas had invested in some bum Florida real estate in the 20s.

So there I was with a cabin in the North Woods, which had always been what Uncle Tomas promised me if I worked hard and saved. And now it was handed to me; but now, I didn't know what the hell to do with it. I don't know anything about fishing. Uncle Tomas talked about Walleye Pike and Muskellunge. I don't even know what they look like. I'm a jazzman not a fisherman. I wonder if Stella would have liked going to the north woods up there near Hayward, Wisconsin. To be honest, I don't know.

For a while I had trouble sleeping. The nights were so hot. No breeze came through the windows. I lay there in my boxer shorts sweating. Outside, it was raining, just dripping, making a sound like water hitting the ground after twisting a wet towel. It was drip dripping from a stuffed up gutter. Sometimes, way far away I could hear some thunder. A few times a car came down the street. Heard the swish of tires on the wet pavement. A thought came as I stared at the dark ceiling. Maybe I was wrong, a jazzman is a fisherman, 'cause music, see, music catches the soul.

Could feel everything on those summer nights: my toes, my beard growing, the damp wrinkled sheet through my back, my heart, the blood rushing through my ears. All of it syncopating. Was I having a heart attack? Then the Bohemian came out in me. I couldn't let myself have no heart attack. I didn't have clean underwear on. I lay there with my hands folded on my chest. If I'd had a rosary wrapped around my fingers, I'd have looked like a stiff in a casket. Still, when my warm spit built up around my tongue, and I had to swallow, by God, I knew I was alive. Knowing that, somehow made me cry, and I cried till I fell asleep. As soon as the sun came up, my eyes blinked open, and the feeling of the night was gone. I felt washed clean. Thoughts about caskets and buying my own plot at the Bohemian National Cemetery disappeared.

Some say the Depression was still going on, but I'll tell you, the factories were hiring. The Chinks and the Japs were fighting because of Marco Polo,[113] but I didn't understand why 'cause I thought Marco Polo invented spaghetti.[114] The point was, they were fighting, and we were making things for the Chinese, see.[115]

Something about the factory I missed. Sure, I missed the money at times, but I missed being with the guys. Musicians, well, we're connected like Siamese twins, but the Chicago worker, well I liked being around that banter. It was music too—rough music, hard drinking, fight on the drop of a hat music. The banter sparked jazz music in my head. Made a composer out me. And the Chicago worker's got this swaggering kind of humor. You got to be around them. So I said to myself, "George, what the hell?" The gigs weren't coming as regular as I wanted, so why not get a factory job again? Get it out of my system. Listen to them workers again to feed my jazz to help me create jazz.

You got your basic two kinds of factory workers, ones who were wiry and strong and had big mouths and ones who were big and had bellies like buchta (yeast raised bun or cake) dough. The first bunch talked about steak and eggs and the other about sweets. The first bunch worked with things like jackhammers or loaded stuff on trucks. They slept good at night and thought they had good jobs. The others, well they complained all the time, about the bosses, the work, their wives, whatever. They did the line jobs—you know, assemble part A into Part B. Now do it again.

But both groups talked about dames. At lunch over garlic dill pickles fished from barrels at the delicatessen, or thick sausage sandwiches on rye that was soaked in grease, or gulping down quarts of chocolate milk it'd go something like, "I found something sweet last weekend," holding his hands way out in front of his chest, mouth bulging with food, "with tits out to here. And she had a face like a Hollywood actress. Couldn't keep her hands off me." The guy looked like somebody shoved in his face, and his ass hung out of his pants, so nobody really believed him. They were stories. That was all. Everybody had big male parts, and the dames all squealed with pleasure, and everybody spoke like experts about the bodies of Negroes and Chinese. The point is, these guys made up the stories to spice up their lives and pepper things up. Without the stories the only things left sometimes were shots and beers.

Anyway, I seen this sign that said there was jobs right away. You know, the usual, come to the plant, go to the employment office, good wages, need men willing to work hard for a good day's wages. I'm thinking, this is just what I was dreaming about. I'm one lucky guy. So the next morning I take a bath and shave and off I go. I'll admit it, I had some flutters in my stomach like I feel when I go on stage.

So I get off the streetcar near the plant that was advertising. I never seen such a commotion. There must be a thousand guys along this here big iron fence around the plant. And they're blocking the main gate, so I'm confused. They're chanting something, but I can't understand. It sounds like a steel forge, "Wah! Wah! Wah!" Their voices are echoing off the front wall of the plant.

Police paddy wagons are running around, and cops got billy clubs out. I go up to one cop and ask, "Excuse me officer, but I'm confused."

He says back, "Well that makes two of us."

"I don't want to cause no trouble," I says, "But I seen in the newspaper an ad that this plant is advertising for jobs and to come here and sign up at the employment office, but the front gate's blocked."

The cop, he gives me this weird smile, and says back pointing to another gate further down where a lot of cops are standing. "You just go in there pal, and they'll take care of you."

So I walk down the street on the opposite side of the crowd to the gate where the cop sent me. As soon as I get to the gate, the crowd starts screaming even louder, and they start rushing to where I am. One of the cops asks me, "You here for a job?"

I shake my head yes. It was hard to hear over the noise. The cop says, "Okay then, we'll walk you in." So two cops start walking me down the sidewalk to a door I see that has "Employment" over it. Underneath it says, "Immediate Openings." So far so good.

Now the crowd is real close, and they're shoving and pushing at other cops, and some of them are spitting—maybe even at me. For what, I'm asking myself. Then I hear them clear for the first time; they're screaming at me, "Scab, scab, scab!"[116] Then I figure it out. The plant's on strike, and I'm crossing the picket line. I ain't no scab! Strange what comes to your mind. I'm thinkin', the apple don't fall far from the tree. Just like Pa, I'm in the line to be a strike breaker. But I got a mind of my own, so I turn to one of the cops and say, "I don't want to cross the picket line. I got to go back." He didn't seem to pay no attention. He looked scared, so I turn to the other cop. Just then the crowd breaks, and they rush us. One guy pushes the cop next to me on to his ass, and I hear him bounce off the pavement. I glance up from the cop just in time to see, I'm not sure what, a 2x4 or an axe handle or something coming at me. Wham!

The next thing I know is my eyes are blinking open; I'm on my back. Bright lights are flashing in front of my eyes. Let me tell you, with each flash, there's this stab of pain, but then, even though the light hurts, I open my eyes. Nobody needed to tell me. I was in a hospital. I was like Pa regarding doctors and hospitals. I gotta get out of here I'm telling myself. I pull myself up on to the edge of the bed. Then I stand up, holding onto the bed rail. First thing I do is puke, and I fell right onto the floor and into my own puke. There's some kind of commotion, and I feel people around me, and then I'm out of it again.

When I came out of it the second time, I couldn't really tell ya. Finally, I remember some doctor comes by my bed and says, "Well, George, didn't think you were going to make it. Nasty knock on the head." Didn't need no doctor to tell me that. Something about fractions, he says. Said it was going to be tough for me. I told him it's always been tough. A jazzman's life is tough. He says the symptoms will go down but probably not disappear. Don't know about no permanent damage. Main thing was to rest a little bit. Can I go home now and rest there, I ask, but he says gotta wait some days on account of my head swelling. How about my music I ask. He said music was good for me. I didn't need no doctor to tell me that either.

So that left me to lay in that hospital bed and stew. Nobody came to visit; nobody knew I was there. I wanted to get word to Jimmy. I daydreamed a lot about Stella by starlight. The cops came by and wanted to know if I wanted to press charges against the guy who whacked me. I said, No. What was the point of that? Told the cops it was a mix-up. Later, Jimmy Nosek told me I was "nuts" to do that, said the guy deserved to burn. Maybe it was the bump on the head, but I didn't have energy for revenge. Are people supposed to feel pain 'cause I feel pain for what they did? No jazz will come out of that.

There was this night nurse by the name of Janice Havelka, a Bohemian gal. She took pity on me, and I don't know why. Maybe because I found out she had a brother who was a musician living out on the West Coast. I guess she missed him, and she saw something of him in me. It's my guess. She made sure my pillow was all fluffed up, and she always fussed over my blankets. Janice was no beauty, but her smile was honest, and she spoke clear, and there wasn't an ounce of fake in her.

When she wasn't too busy, she'd come by to chat about the small things. She knew about kolaczky. She bathed me, too. I remember this one time she washed my sad big feet. All that was bothering me seemed to leave me, and I swear I saw the guy in the wheelchair sitting across from me, smiling. There he was, propped up, no arms or legs like a washboard. He seemed happy, and if he could be happy, so could I.

When I got a little better, Janice brought me to the big shower room at the end of the hall. It was late at night and quiet except for the sound of someone off in the distance moaning. It was a hospital after all. She soaped me all up and scrubbed my head and back with a wash cloth. The warm water felt good pouring over my head and down my back. Janice soaped up the cloth again, but this time she holds my personal part in the cloth, and she begins to rub it back and forth. I don't know how long it lasted, but I don't have enough education to explain how it felt. I watched what came out swirl around the drain and disappear. Then I leaned my head against the shower wall and bawled like a baby for the longest time. And Janice stayed with me and gently rubbed my back.

The day I got out of the hospital was near Easter, and it was a beautiful spring morning. It hurt to walk, but I walked anyway. I was in part of the Dago neighborhood near where I lived. They were having a procession. So there's these guys and women all dressed up in Biblical style. And then here comes Jesus, and he's a real good-looking guy they must have picked special to play the part. Long black curly hair, big muscles, the whole works. Other people are playing their parts, jeering at him but sometimes laughing too. Well, over his shoulder, he's got this big wooden cross made out of 4x6s, and he's making as if he's dragging it down the street. But see, on the bottom of this cross is a big metal wheel. The cross has got a wheel on it. What the hell!

So I finally get home, and what do you think, the brother and sister, the Bobbsey Twins,[117] are waddling out of their house. Holding hands at that. Imagine that at their age! I says to myself, "Ah hovno! (shit)"

Right away, 'cause they can never keep their mouths shut they peep up. "Hey Nepras, where the hell you been?"

"Now what Czerny?" I says back.

"Get that shit yard of yours cut, will ya? What the hell, you're hurting the property values."

Imagine that, I think, here's a brother and sister living like they was married, and I'm hurting the property values. I wave to them, "Yeah, yeah, yeah."

The blimp of a sister is just standing there with her hands on her hips. Then she starts laughin'. She's got a big gold tooth. So I'm lookin' at her, and she takes her finger and twirls it around the side of her head, meaning crazy, see, and then she points the finger at me. The whole thing was making me dizzy, and my head was starting to pound, so I do the only thing I can, and unlock the door and go in the house. It stunk inside.

I cleaned out the icebox. Nothing in there even looked like food anymore. The smell of the stuff I used to clean it reminded me of the hospital, and I felt sick again. In fact I felt really sick, nauseated, and dizzy, and flashing lights, so I went to bed. Everything was there just the way I left it before I went off to apply for that factory job. I went into some kind of deep sleep with strange dreams.

In one dream I remember, I'm playing the Conn, but the sound that comes out is that growling and whispering sound of Ben Webster on the sax.[118] There's a woman in the dreams too, but I don't know who she is. Mostly she's got her back to me, and every time she turns around a bright light keeps me from seeing her face, but she sings something beautiful, not jazz but still beautiful. Maybe it was what we say in Bohemian, ukolebovka (lullaby). A lot of the dreams scared me, but I don't remember what of. But this woman singing was like the drugs they gave me at the hospital. Didn't want it to stop, and I would have been glad to spend forever listening to it. The next day I woke up late. I was so thirsty I drank four glasses of water.

But that ukolobovka, little pieces of it stayed with me for days. I tried to play it on the trumpet. Then I remembered. You know I've told you a lot about Pa, but dreaming that ukolobovka, brought back a memory of him that was buried from so long ago—this memory is of being so tiny that I'm looking over the shoulder of Pa—he must have been carrying me—and he's singing something in Bohemian, I think it was. Was I crying? I think I was. And I think it was this ukolobovka. Now I pray when I go to sleep I will dream and hear this woman sing it again.

Chapter 17

Sharps, Flats, and Blues Notes

I went back to that shed near the rail yard. I burned scraps of wood in a metal drum there to keep warm. And nobody bothered me. I played again, but it wasn't the same. For a week, every time I tried to blow a note, my head rang like a bell with pain, and it seemed the train whistles complained back at me. My head was sharp and the whistles flat. Coal smoke from the engines snuck inside the shed. Still, I played on. The notes weren't coming. It was a jumble, see. Sometimes I sat on the floor of the shed, staring off into nowhere until my butt was as cold as a well digger's ass.

Every once in a while I get this urge to eat an onion sandwich. I get the baba rye from Jana's Bakery, lather it up with good butter, and put a couple of big slices of sweet onion on it. Nothing tastes better when I'm in the mood. It's like my body is telling me I need it. Some instinct. Well, it was suddenly that way with this urge to start walking again. So even though I was dizzy at times, I started walking at night just like the old days. Car headlights bothered me, and horns made me grab my skull, but the walking started to drain bad things out of me. I can't be more exact than that.

As luck would have it, I was walking downtown in the loop somewhere, and I cut down an alley 'cause the lights were bothering me on the street, and in this alley I find myself behind some theater, I forget the name, and I run into this Negro man. At first I didn't recognize him on account of the light being so dim, but he knows me right off. "George," he says.

Even from that I knew the voice from the gravel in his throat. It was Cecil, a trombonist I played with a few time in the old days and got to know over beers discussing jazz. He was out back of the theater having a smoke. We sized each other up and knew right off neither of us was going through the best of times.

In the old days, Cecil had liked the ponies, and I had bailed him out of a couple of jams with a sawbuck or two. He was a good musician though, but he was one of those guys that couldn't read the music. Cecil was in old clothes, so I knew he wasn't performing there. He tells me he does maintenance.

But then he gets real intense with me. His leathery face is up close to mine, and his eyes have a shine to them. He says, "George, man, you gots to listen to this music they gonna play tonight. I been hearing it for two nights, man."

"So I says, "What is it?"

He says back, "Some cat named Debussy wrote it."

Well, you can imagine what's going through my mind. All the memories of Stella come back. I had pushed music like Debussy out of my mind like so much from back then, so I could forget and get over things.

"George," he says, "I can get you in."

"Hey Cecil," I says, "I don't want to get you in trouble, man."

"No problem amigo. I owe you, man. You helped old Cecil out when I was jammed up."

"Forget about that, Cecil."

"No man, I don't forget. Come on in man, and then we be square."

Well the long and short of it is Cecil got me in, and he hid me in a corner where I could see and listen. The music grabbed me so strong I could barely stay on my feet. I don't know if it was because of Stella or what. There was this piece of music, Dances S something[119] that for a while gave me back all I have ever lost. There's this harp, see. My head was so different since I'd gotten it whacked. But the harp, instead of ringing my head sent soft tones like warm rain to the places where it hurt.

After, I told Cecil that getting a chance to listen was the best gift anyone had given me in years. I took Cecil to an all-night joint for a bowl of soup, and I talked him into a hamburger. We talked about old times in the clubs and where jazz was headed. Cecil could tell a great story. I hope he tells his story in a book some day. So many stories get lost. His laugh made me laugh.

A good talk like with Cecil has a way of making the world right, but the world wasn't right. The Paper Hanger[120] got Lloyd George and the rest of them Europeans[121] to sell Bohemia down the river.[122] The neighborhood was really in shock. It's all anybody talked about at the butcher and at Jana's. There were parades against the Germans. I remember on some of the signs was "Mnichouska zrada" (Munich betrayal). A blind man could see how bad things were getting. Agnes Benesh was all over the neighborhood crying, saying she was related to Edvard Benesh,[123] but I don't know. She was putting on such a production. This was the first I ever heard about it. I think she just wanted to be part of all the talk. Everybody was talking about Edvard Benesh.

The worst part of the whole thing is how when some people saw my name and knew it was Bohunk they said things like, "Oh, you're the man without a country." I'm an American. My country is America. What were they talking about? Some meant it as a joke. And let me tell you I was sorry about the Bohemians living under Hitler that SOB, and I'm glad he got his and all his cronies. But Chicago was my home, and America was my country.

The war came when the Japs sneak attacked us, but we were going to take care of the Paper Hanger first. Now the factories were running three shifts. The city collected old pots and pans for the war to help the boys in the trenches.[124] Everybody started Victory Gardens.[125] I put out tomatoes, but I got some kind of bugs that ate them up. They had a gasoline shortage but who had a car? Old man Sevcek was an air-raid warden, but no bombs dropped on Chicago. All he did when he was on duty was lose his shirt playing poker. Some families kept stars in the windows. That meant you had a boy in the service. The Bluma boy got shot up pretty bad. He was a nose gunner on a B-26. Charlie Smedlaha's boy got decorated for blowin' up a Jap pillbox. At least nobody used gas, which would have made Zeke happy. Zeke always preached that the next war was gonna be the end of everything: poison gas, germs, ray guns, and the like. Instead, it was the usual kind of war until it ended with an atomic bomb.

The twist for us Bohunks was in the First World War America fought Bohemia, but in the second, we were on the same side. I always wondered in the first world war whether Chicago Bohemians had actually duked it out with Prague Bohemians, but Zeke and his bunkmates said in a war, you hardly ever see the enemy up close, and when you do, you're busy bayoneting each other and don't have time to ask 'em about where they're from.

Well, I wanted to do my bit. I stood in line to volunteer, but I got counted out real fast. Seems I was too old.[126] And then there was the bump on the head I took, and they said it showed up on my qualification test, but I don't know how.

I figured I could at least play in one of those military bands. Talk about going in a full circle 'cause there was that relative who played in the Kaiser's military band back in Bohemia. Maybe Kryl was still around leading a military band. Then I thought, nah, he was too old wherever he was. But the Army didn't want me for that either.

So okay, but I heard they were hiring for the torpedo factory on Roosevelt Road not so far from Cicero, just a couple of miles west. I'm the first to admit that I don't know the first thing about torpedoes. In Cicero if you said torpedo, a person would think you were talking about one of Al Capone's hit men. Hell, I'm a jazz cornetist, but when your nation calls, well then you learn something new. Fortunately, they had plenty of torpedo experts, and they offered me a job cleaning up.

Well, I put everything I had into it. Sometimes I worked two shifts. My cornet practicing dropped off, but it was for the war effort. Anyway, that bang on the head still bothered me and my playing, so giving it a pause was probably the right thing to do. You can't push jazz. I kept the Conn polished though. I did no clubbing, so I was only listening to jazz on records. Kept spinning a record of Bix playing Davenport Blues. I wore out the record during the war because I played it so many times I had the sheet music too. The light blue cover was faded a little and dog-eared. You know I was in that recording studio when he made that record.[127] It made me think of good times and the first electric feel of jazz when it caught my soul.

Time passed fast in the war. Kind of funny because that don't seem right what with all the death. It passed without a fuss. One day melted into the next. Was there and gone. Not even a back beat. In some ways, not worrying about how my music career was going took some weight off my shoulders. Hustling for the next gig is tough. I know all you jazzmen can appreciate that. The job was like the one I had at the Hawthorne Park Race Track. Sweeping up is sweeping up. The difference was this job had a purpose. The race track job when I think back on it, made me sad. The whole thing seemed such a waste, losing your money betting on a nag. But the torpedo plant—sending them torpedoes out to the boys to sink Jap ships and such—well that meant something, and I'm proud I played my part.

Chapter 18

Bebop[128]—The Final Testament

Who says you have to have four beats to a measure? Why not eight beats or ten beats? Why not six-six time? Why not a cornet you play with a reed? Didn't guys like Clark Terry[129] put the flugelhorn[130] into jazz? Dizzy Gillespie,[131] oh my God, how about his bent trumpet? That changed everything! How cool is cool? I remember going to the movies for twelve hours one day just to watch the newsreel that had this part about Dizzy with his beret and black-rimmed glasses looking like a Beatnik and with his bent horn, playing, I forget what, I think it was *Night in Tunisia*.[132] They say Thelonius Monk "bends notes." All them classical long hair types from the symphonies go to Harlem, I'm told, just to listen to these master jazzmen. In jazz you can invent what you want. And in Bebop jazz the inventions can come from outer space and get beamed back on Sputnik.[133] You get to make your world all over again.

Late at night, in the bedroom I'd had since I was a kid, I'd lay on my bed in the dark, and listen to the radio. The notes of Bebop danced around inside me. Sometimes I dozed off and had some lively strange dreams. Bebop always played in the background. In one dream I had my own sextet, and Charlie Parker was my saxophonist, and we played a gig at the castle in Krumlov. Stella made her appearances, starlight in the background, the beauty of my music making her smile. Music was everything in that dark room. The wild improvisations of Bebop made me feel sometimes like I was floating over the bed, and my head didn't even hurt. Once, in my half sleep, I saw Bix. He waved to me. And I wondered if Bebop was the path to heaven.

So I studied Bebop the way Bix studied Debussy. You got to be fast to play Bebop. But I had a lot of years of apprenticeship. That two-way pump I talked about before was working. Breathing it all into my heart and out again in my own special way. One day I picked up my horn and started blowing Bebop. My fingers moved over those mother-of-pearl valves like the garter snakes that used to swish through the prairie grass.

So many times in my life everything seemed far away. Like that night with Bix hanging on my shoulder drunk, us staggering down the street that seemed to disappear into nowhere. I recollect how the production line at the plant was the same way. It all disappeared into nowhere. Or the line of workers going through the gate at the Western back when I sold newspapers as a kid. Then there was that hall in the hospital where they had old Zeke cooped up, vanishing off beyond where I could see. But now, Bebop changed all that. I'd come to the end of the road. It's where all the roads I'd been on finally came together. It was what I was looking for since the day Kryl let me hold that trumpet in the sunroom.

Still, Bebop was hard for me. When you hear one of the Bebop greats like Charlie Parker on the sax, Dizzy on the trumpet, Max Roach[134] on the drums, you want to say forget it. They're so good you ask yourself what's the point in even trying. They're in this separate league like Bix was.

One day I met this guy who saw Charlie Parker play, I think at Minton's[135] in New York, which is supposed to be a famous place for hearing Bebop. Well, this guy says something like, "I was a clarinetist and saxophonist. I graduated Jewel yard,"[136] That's a famous music school I figure something like what Kryl had but bigger. "So I wasn't without some talent. I'm sitting in that club waiting to hear 'Bird',[137] and he was something like an hour late getting to the club. Well, the group's playing to fill time when Bird walks in the back of the club. His coat and hat's still on, but he starts playin', and as he's walking to the front of the club I'm thinking to myself how damn good he was. The minute that song was over, I decided to put down my sax forever. No sense trying. I'd seen perfection."

So I thought maybe I should start to pray about all this 'cause the changes had me so confused. I spent time at the parish in the quiet of the back pews. Usually, I had my trumpet or cornet case with me because I was usually over at the shed practicing before I stopped in. Having one of my horns with me was always a great comfort. I discovered that if you prayed to the statues especially along one of the side altars, and you concentrated real hard, the statues would give you a little smile or a wink. Sometimes I could see them move their lips.

Often, what I looked for when I prayed would come to me later, and that's the way it was about music, and what I was trying to do and where I was trying to go. The point wasn't to be better than those guys like Bird. It was only about what came out of my horn. I could only give it everything I had which was all I'd been doing anyway. The rest wasn't up to me. But I've said that before. So, every day, when I practiced, I tried to get those greats out of my mind, and I worried instead about the air that went into and out of that silver Conn. And I was happy. And I was peaceful.

Other things began to change too. Jimmy Nosek moved with his wife into a house out in Brookfield he said was between a bowling alley and a liquor store. With that arrangement, Jimmy must have felt like he had died and gone to heaven. Jimmy mentioned he manages a warehouse. When he told me about his gig the first time, I thought he said, "whorehouse." I didn't even blink. Funny, Brookfield, remember, was where Ma and I went to pick onions, but there's no farms in Brookfield anymore Jimmy says.

Then one Saturday morning coming back from the savings and loan where I kept my money I hear this squeaking behind me. I knew exactly what it was 'cause I'd heard it most of my life. It had to be Mrs. Wotschka's two-wheeled shopping cart. When I was a kid, if it was summer and the windows were open, and I heard that squeaking, I'd peek from behind the living room curtains, and watch Mrs. Wotschka pass. She had pretty lips and bright shining eyes, and she had these ankles, see.

It made me happy to hear something familiar from the neighborhood. I couldn't help myself. I stopped and turned around. It wasn't Mrs. Wotschka; it was an old lady pulling the cart bent over the way old ladies get, like she had a big hump. But then something about the woman was like Mrs. Wotschka, so I took the chance, and asked, "Mrs. Wotschka?"

The old lady stops, but she keeps her head down. I can see her brow kind of wrinkle up, and her eyes look up to see who's calling. Her voice squeaks like a mistake on a clarinet. "Who are you?

"I am George, the Nepras boy. Are you Mrs. Wotschka?"

"Yeah," she says back, but it's still hard for me to believe. "You're the Nepras boy?"

"Ano," I says in Bohemian. "So how's it going?" not knowing what else to say.

"Phooey," she says back. "Going, nothing's going except my hearing. I can't even scratch my back on a door frame no more."

I tell her I was sorry to hear that and offered to bring her some kolaczky or something, but she says, "Phooey, what am I gonna do with the kolaczky. I can't eat no poppy seed, the doctor said, on account of divertiyois [sic]."[138]

So I suggest cheese ones and she says, "Gives me constipation." So I excuse myself, offer one last time if I can carry her packages or something, but at the end, we just go off separate ways, but then she stops again and shouting in her crackling voice I could barely hear over the wind. "You know they're almost to the water tower!"

"What is?" I ask her.

She mouths some word then says, "Property values are gonna go down."

Well, I walked to the water tower that night. When I was a boy and Mrs. Wotschka still had pretty ankles, I thought the tower was a castle ruin. I thought that castle guarded the border of the neighborhood like the one in Krumlov must have done. Now in modern times at night, it looked to me like an atomic bomb cloud.[139] It had been a while since I had been there, and I was curious about what Mrs. Wotschka meant. I discovered Negroes lived on the streets east of the water tower now. Before, only Bohemians lived there. Nothing stays the same.

The next morning I suddenly wanted to see the apartment building where Bohumir Kryl had lived. I was anxious like I had an itch that had to be scratched. He had been out of my life for so long. I guess the connection of Kryl and my life with Stella made me not want to go near the place. I didn't want to relive those memories. But somehow, just then I burned to go back to where so much started for me. With so much changing around me, I needed something I could count on.

But by the time I got there, I couldn't believe it. It was a spring day, just like the first time I went there for that first cornet lesson, but that was all that was the same. There was no streetcar, so I had to take a bus. When Kryl had lived there, it was a neighborhood for swells. Now it was run down. Poor colored folk were there. 'Cause a Negro man moves in, we all run away? All my life I had seen that. What are all these people afraid of? And from the Negro who brought jazz up the river from New Orleans! I was getting hard looks from young toughs. I want to shout, "I'm George Nepras, I was on a bandstand jamming after hours with colored folk when no bands was integrated!" What would Stella think? I was so sad when I got home, I didn't get up for two days. And in my heart, I have to admit if I'm gonna be honest to all you young jazzmen out there, I resented those Negroes in Kryl's old neighborhood. Nothing against them personally, only I wanted that place just the way it had been.

One bright spring day, practicing in the shed, it came to me to ask, where did the notes I blew go? Were they gone forever? Could nobody ever hear them? Did that corrugated metal dump of a place soak them up like a towel? Maybe there was some way they could be stored up because I'd be real interested to hear those notes I first blew when I started to know jazz. But then I thought, well maybe every note I blow is really bits from all the notes I already blew. Maybe the notes are real heavy, and maybe they all bounce around like a baseball when it's whacked into the left field corner in Comiskey Park.

Those thoughts were on my mind when I was walking down on the lakefront near the Prudential Building.[140] I hear this young fella, maybe he was 25 or so with blond hair practically hanging over his eyes, wearing clothes I didn't recognize as coming from Chicago, and he's speaking Bohemian. He's asking himself, "So where's the museum?"

So my Bohemian wasn't what it was, and it was never any good, but I had enough to say, "Je to tam. (It's over there.)"

Well, this kid practically falls over. The Bohemian starts pouring out of him.

"Slow down," I says to him, and finally, after this kid gets over the excitement, and is convinced I'm not in the secret police, we figure out English is best, so we take a walk over to a coffee shop I know. I explain how the teachers told us kids how speaking Bohemian would just hold you back in America. This kid corrects me and says the language is "Cesky jazyk." I tell him he's crazy. He just blinks at me. So I tell him again how I got my ears boxed if I spoke the old language.

"Why hold you back?" he asks me.

I says back, "How the hell should I know?"

He asks me what I do, and I tell him I'm a jazzman, a syncopator, and I find out he already knows about Miles Davis, and he already knows all about American Rock and Roll. His name is Karel Cerny, and he's from the Pilsen in Bohemia and not the Pilsen neighborhood we lived in when I was a little kid.

I ask him if he was a farmer 'cause if he is, Chicago's the wrong place. I tell him most of the Bohemian farmers went to Wisconsin and Nebraska. For a while, he don't say nothing. He just blinks. Finally he says that he's an engineer, so I tell him about the rail yards near the house. And he blinks some more.

I tell him about Jana's Bakery and the good kolaczky. Then I say something like, "Of course I'm sure the kolaczky is better in Bohemia."

And he says back, "George, nobody's thinking right now in Czechoslovakia about kolaczky! They are thinking about the great hovadina (bullshit) otherwise called great socialist experiment." He pauses a second and then he reaches over and grabs my shirt. I think for a minute Karel was gonna take a poke at me. "George," he says to me, "sitting in this place, smelling the food. I'm so hungry, please sir, can you buy me something to eat?"

"Sure," I says back, "I don't let nobody go hungry, just don't stretch the material, kid." So I order a cheeseburger and fries and a malt. He liked it 'cause he vacuumed up the food. He tells me he hadn't eaten nothin' in more than a day. Karel tried to whisper, but when he starts telling me his story, there's so much emotion it comes out of him like a hiss, like somebody yanking an air hose free.

At first I thought he was a tourist, but he says, "I'm no tourist. I escaped Czechoslovakia. After running for days I swam the Thaya River."[141]

"Escape," I says, "Why didn't you just leave like all the Bohunks here?"

He grabs his head and pulls his hair. "It's prison George. I was at the Technical University in Brno, and I was saying things the authorities didn't like, so I had to get out."

"You mean these Communists?"

"I mean *gangsteri,* thugs you say here. That's all they are. First I got to Krumlov."

"Krumlov!" I practically jumped out of my seat. "That's where my Ma's family's from. Did you see the castle?"

"See it, George, I slept in the shadows of it while I was escaping. Krumlov is maybe 25 kilometers from Brno." He goes on. Well, I'm listening close now.

"And from there I go to the river, maybe 30 more kilometers, almost nothing to eat, I couldn't trust no one. At night, I get to Austria, almost drowned and starving. For while I live in refugee center, but I get visa to America." Then he says, "George I can do anything. I'm civil engineer, but I can fix cars; I can teach; I can fix machines."

"Well I don't know. I'll try to help."

"It's big insane asylum back there. I'm worried about my family."

"But at least the food's good. Pork. Dumplings, sauerkraut, svickova, Muscovy duck."

"George, nobody eats like that now. That's old style, George. Many of these things are hard to get. What are they doing to my family?" I see tears. And then suddenly he stands up. "I'll go back. Maybe they won't do anything to my mother if I go back." With that he just runs out of the place. Doesn't say another word. Everybody's staring. I'm getting the eye from the owner. I guess he thinks I'm gonna bolt. So I say, "Hey, bring the check."

By the time I get outside, there's no sign of him. But that talk with Karel really changed tempo on me. The score of my life starts rolling backwards, measure by measure, the good things and the bad. Some of it made me shake to think about. The dizziness came back, and I was already wearing the dark glasses all day as it was to stop my head hurting.

The way I figure it Bohemia alone had changed four times in my life. And it wasn't none too good changes neither. Empires, Nazis, Commies, what the hell is this? I'm thinking maybe time's running out for Bohemia and maybe it's running out for me too. Everything felt mixed up. Maybe God loved me; maybe God hated me. Maybe it was about time to start wrapping up the jazz project. I looked in the mirror, whoa, I wasn't looking the same either. I was changing just like the neighborhood, and Bohemia, and jazz.

It came to me that I had to teach you young jazzmen. Had to pass on what I have. See, things didn't work out that I got a nice lady to marry or kids to raise. I guess that was my fault. Everything happened so fast. But I have what I have. And I want to give it to you all.

Sometimes when I leave the house with my cornet case, kids follow me like I was some Pied Piper. They point me out to each other. So full of life they are, and they filled my heart with happiness. Sometimes they'd ask for autographs.

I always oblige them, but the mothers sometimes notice me with the kids and call them back. The mothers look worried for my privacy. I always call to them and say things like, "It's okay. I like kids. It's important to encourage kids 'cause the kid you're talking to might be the next Miles Davis."

I have to tell you the old New Orleans music is calling this Bohemian kid. It's calling me to a home, to a city I don't even know. Still, I knew that New Orleans was the heart behind everything I set out to do. I'm comforted by the thought that if I got on a raft on the Chicago River, I'd come to the Des Plaines River, and then whatever river, and then eventually go down to the Mississippi and float down that vein, waving to St. Louis on the way, and end up in New Orleans, "Land of Dreams", as Satchmo says in the song.[142] Never been to New Orleans, but I think that's where I'm headed when I put my Conn away. Some place down there an old banjo player told me was called the Elysium Fields[143] which he said was paradise.

So you young jazzmen, you syncopators, I've told you my story, and I've never lied. You can see what it took me to make it in jazz. Uncle Tomas said you have to keep your nose clean and work hard, and it will come to you. It's not easy, but you can do it, and I want you to do it. I want your hearts to be as filled as mine and as happy as I turned out. What I have had I give to you. I guess that's all there is I have to say. It's done.

Notes

BY CHARLES SVOBODA

    1   I have been unable to uncover records of where and when George was born. Cook County, which includes Chicago, has no record of his birth. I was able to establish that he finished the eighth grade in 1912, which suggests birth in 1898. Most likely, he was born between 1897 and 1900 somewhere other than Chicago. In my imagination I see him born on a ship from Europe to America. This, however, seems to contradict George's assertion that his father was somehow involved in strike-breaking during the McCormick factory strike of 1886. Unless his biological father died, it is unlikely he could have been born before arriving in Chicago and yet his father was working here at least a decade earlier. George's reference here to his "heart playing music for forty-two years" is also problematic. A forty-two year span would mean he began playing in 1920, and as the story unfolds, the reader will realize he began considerably before that date, probably 1912. I assume one of three things: the dates are incorrect, his calculations are confused, or he is referring to when he was first introduced to jazz.

    2   George's references to Bohemia are often confused. Bohemia is a province of Czechoslovakia and a former province of the Austro-Hungarian Empire. Prague is the capital of Bohemia and the capital of the current communist regime in Czechoslovakia. Bohemian is not, as George asserts, a separate language. Bohemians speak Czech. In Chicago, the majority of immigrants from what is known today as Czechoslovakia were from Bohemia, so there is a tendency for Czechs to use Bohemian and Czech interchangeably. Although the precise number of Bohemians who came to America is uncertain because many Bohemians were registered as Austrians, estimates from 1848 on place the number at 250,000. Bohemian immigration peaked in 1906 with the arrival of 13,000.

    3   The McCormick Reaper Plant on the edge of the largely Czech Pilsen neighborhood produced some of the country's first generation of automated farm machinery. In 1886, plant workers struck over wage cuts, and the company introduced strike breakers, precipitating the infamous Haymarket Square riots.

4   Pilsen is located on the near south side of Chicago and was aptly named because of the large percentage of Czechs living there in the latter part of the 19th and early 20th centuries.

5   Bohunk is a slang term to mean Bohemian. Usually its meaning is deprecatory but can also be self-effacing or humorous.

6   After passage of the 18th Amendment in 1919, "Speakeasies" surfaced as private and technically illegal clubs that sold alcohol of varying quality during Prohibition. These clubs were often mafia-run, and associated with both prostitution and the rise of the new "hot music": jazz. It was in the speakeasies and dance halls of 1920's Chicago that jazz became wildly popular and crossed racial lines. .

7   Blues notes are sometimes called "worried notes" by musicians. They are flatter and about a semitone lower.

8   William John Evans (1929-present) Considered by some the most influential jazz pianist in the post-World War II era. His impressionist style has been a major influence on a whole generation of jazz pianists.

9   Coleman Hawkins (1904-present) One of the first prominent jazz tenor saxophonists who had a great deal of influence on subsequent jazz greats like Lester Young. His recording of *Body and Soul* is often viewed by musicologists as the key transitional piece between Swing and Bebop.

10   Dago is a pejorative term for Italians.

11   Ernest "Punch" Miller: (1894-present) Dixieland jazz trumpeter arrived in Chicago in the 1920s and played with Jelly Roll Morton.

12   Bohumir Kryl (1875-1961) was born on May 2 in Hradec near Hradec Kralove in Bohemia. He was considered one of the great cornet virtuosos of his time. During the 1890's he played in John Phillip Sousa's band and conducted an Army band during WWI. He originally immigrated to America by joining the circus as an acrobat. Kryl was also a sculptor. The Conn Instrument Company appeared to have been a major promoter of Kryl.

13   John Philip Sousa was also known as the "March King". He conducted the Marine Corps Band, which became legendary and known as "The President's Own." Sousa composed iconic American marches such as *Stars and Stripes Forever.*

14   The Bohemian National Cemetery was founded in 1877 and is associated with the "Free Thinkers" movement.

15 Comiskey Park is the home of the Chicago White Sox baseball team and is on the south side of Chicago. The team tends to be more popular with working-class Chicagoans than its rival, the Chicago Cubs, who play on the north side.

16 *Saturday Night at the Fights* was one of the earliest broadcast programs on TV. Every broadcast featured a prize fight.

17 The ZCBJ or "Zapadni Cesko Bratrska Jednota" (Western Czech Fraternal Organization) was founded in 1897 and supported free-thinking ideas in stark contrast to the teachings of the Catholic Church. In the cities, the organization was suspected of association with radical labor movements.

18 Kolaczky literally means a small cake. In Chicago, kolaczky specifically came to mean a small round or sometimes folded-over dough with a filling in the middle. The dough is closer to a cookie or butter biscuit than cake. The filling typically is prune, apricot, sweetened poppy seed, or cheese. In Chicago, the singular kolaczky was used interchangeably as a plural.

19 Kolac means cake, but in Chicago was more defined as an open-faced coffee cake. As George describes, it can be topped with any number of ingredients. It was typically eaten in the morning.

20 Houska, which means small rolls, came to mean in Chicago a loaf of an egg-rich raisin bread.

21 Babovka. or fancy cake. In Chicago it was more commonly known as "Baba Rye", a large round loaf of soft rye bread.

22 Earl Randolph "Bud" Powell (1924-present) was born in Harlem and is an influential Bebop pianist.

23 *Svornorst, Spravedlnost, Denni Hlasatel: Harmony, Justice, Daily Herald*. These were three of the many Czech language newspapers available to Chicago's immigrant population.

24 *Svornost* was a leftist labor newspaper.

25 Sokol means falcon in Czech. This was a youth movement founded in Prague in 1862 and was popular in the Czech communities of Chicago. Its thrust was gymnastics but it also offered classes and lectures particularly about Czech history.

26 St. Adelbert is the name of a famous church in Prague.

27 Antonin Dvorak (1841-1904), perhaps the greatest Czech composer, spent 1892-1895 in America. Dvorak conducted his *8th Symphony* at Chicago's Columbia

Exposition in 1893. Several of Dvorak's relatives had immigrated to Iowa. He also directed from 1892-5, The National Conservatory of Music in New York.

28   *Stella by Starlight* (1944) Performed by virtually all the jazz greats, most notably Miles Davis, Charlie Parker, and Stan Getz.

29   Chesney Henry "Chet" Baker Jr. (1929-present) Known for his mellow jazz trumpet and vocals. A leading figure in the "West Coast Jazz" or "Cool Jazz." Chet has struggled with drug addiction.

30   Vienna was the capital of the Austro-Hungarian Empire of which Bohemia was a province and Prague the provincial capital. It is probable that Mr. Vraz lived in Vienna during the "Jugendstil" period, which was a time of immense intellectual, political, and artistic development.

31   Cesko-Slovanska Podporujici Spolecnost (CSPS) This benevolent society served the Czech community with a variety of social services and was particularly helpful in providing support for immigrants.

32   George is likely referring to the song, *Way Down Yonder in New Orleans*. It was written by John Layton and lyrics by Henry Creamer for the 1922 musical, *Spice*.

> "*Way down yonder in New Orleans*
> *In the land of dreamy scenes*
> *There's a garden of Eden . . .*
> *Oh! Won't you give your lady fair a little smile*
> *You bet your life you'll linger there . . .*
> *There's heaven right here on earth*
> *Way down yonder in New Orleans.*"

33   The event that precipitated World War I.

34   The Eastland capsized at the pier as it got ready to depart for the Western's picnic on July 24, 1915. It remains the worst ship disaster on the Great Lakes, with over 800 fatalities, most of whom were employees of Western Electric and were ethnic Czechs.

35   Germans

36   The British passenger ship, *Lusitania*, was sunk by U-Boat 20 off the Irish coast on May 7, 1915. 1,198 people died, many of whom were Americans.

37   George has his dates wrong. The Great Influenza Pandemic began in 1918 and ended in 1920. As many as 675,000 people died, and an estimated 28% of the U.S. population contracted the disease.

38   Sonny Rollins: (1930-present) Born in New York and considered one of the most influential jazz saxophonists in America. He has worked with Bud Powell and Max Roach and other Bop musicians and is a composer in his own right.

39   Chicago's 1919 race riots began on July 27, 1919 and ended in early August. More than a dozen people were killed and hundreds injured. They represent the worst racial violence in the city's history. Competition for scarce jobs between ethnic Irish and the increasing number of Negro migrants from the southern states appears the underlying cause. The precipitating event was an incident at a Lake Michigan beach that ended in police arresting a Negro, but not arresting any whites.

40   By troops George means the National Guard. More than 600 were called up to help the police quell the violence.

41   Polack is a derogatory term for someone from Poland.

42   As best as I can determine, George had wandered into the infamous area of Chicago's south side called the "Stroll", known for open drinking, prostitution, dance cabarets, and jazz clubs. infused with the new hot music, jazz. . In my research I have been unable to find a reference to a club at that time called the "Highlight", so I suspect George was referring to the "Elite Café".

43   I was unable to establish whether "King" Oliver, one of if not the greatest early jazz cornetists, ever played at the Elite at this time. He was certainly in demand in Chicago.. The Dreamland Café and Lincoln Gardens were his main venues.

44   George is certainly referring to the Mississippi River.

45   Louis Armstrong (1901-present) Satchmo, or Pops, has perhaps the single greatest influence of any musician on the development of jazz. His charismatic stage presence and inventive cornet and trumpet playing has led to stardom around the world.

46   George is clearly referring to the incident on December 1, 1955 in Montgomery, Alabama when Rosa Parks refused to move to the Negro-only section of the bus. Her refusal sparked the Montgomery bus boycott led by Martin Luther King. King led a march last year on Washington for jobs and equality. An estimated 250,000 people participated.

47   Anton Cermak (1873-1933) was the mayor of Chicago from 1931 to 1933. He arrived from modern day Czechoslovakia in 1874. He is considered the father

of Chicago's Democratic machine. He was shot in Miami while meeting President Franklin Roosevelt on February 15, 1933. Cermak allegedly said to Roosevelt, "I'm glad it was me and not you." He died of his wounds on March 6th. Numerous rumors abound regarding the shooting. Some said he never made the remark to Roosevelt. Cermak had bitterly opposed Roosevelt's nomination. Many feel Cermak was the actual target of the assassination, and the hit had been arranged by the Chicago mob for Cermak's ruthless pursuit of Mafia kingpin, Frank Nitti.

48 The "Raggedy Pants Brigade" refers to the Marine 4th Brigade composed of the Fifth and Sixth Regiments that fought at the battle of Belleau Wood June 6-26, 1918. Belleau Wood fits mightily in Marine Corps lore. When a French officer suggested withdrawing, a Marine Captain famously answered, "Retreat Hell, we just got here." The French government honored the Marines for their exceptional bravery by renaming Belleau Wood, "Bois de la Brigade Marine".

49 John Coltrane, aka "Trane" (1926-present). A leader of the Bebop movement. Known for his spiritual interpretation, he is one of America's top contemporary jazz saxophonists. It is noteworthy that despite George's interest in traditional New Orleans style jazz, he demonstrates keen appreciation for contemporary jazz greats who are taking jazz in entirely different directions.

50 A thoroughbred horse race track in Cicero that opened in 1891.

51 George was referring to the "Roaring Twenties" and raccoon coats as symbols of a decade of rapid prosperity following the end of WWI and America's rising industrial influence. It was a time of rising promiscuity as well. Raccoon coats were a trend among college students, particularly those from prosperous families with disposable income to spend on indulgences.

52 The Austin High Gang was a group of young white musicians who attended Austin High School on Chicago's West side and are acknowledged as having a major influence on what was to be called the "Chicago sound". Jimmy McPartland on Cornet, Frank Teschemacher on Clarinet, and Bud Freeman on Tenor Sax were its most noteworthy members. Many of Chicago's famous jazz musicians were associated with the Austin High Gang and include: Eddie Condon, Mezz Mezzrow, Benny Goodman, and Gene Krupa (also of Czech descent).

53 Leon "Bix" Beiderbecke (1903-31) A self-taught legendary jazz cornet and trumpet player who was considered ahead of his time. The first truly influential white jazz musician, he is often paired with Louis Armstrong as two of the great early pioneers of jazz who popularized this musical form. He first recorded with the famous Wolverines and then later played in the Paul Whiteman band, which was recognized as the best in the country.

54   Sonny Clark (1931-63) Since he recently passed away, it seems that George was affected by his death. I have speculated about whether there could be a connection between Clark's death and George's disappearance, but I have not found any evidence to suggest a connection. I have also been unable to establish whether George had a personal relationship with Clark. Clark was a pianist of the bop generation and inspiration for jazz pianist, Bill Evans. *Leapin' and Lopin'* was on the Blue Note label in 1961.

55   Emmett Hardy (1903-25) Grew up in Algiers, Louisiana which is the true home of the birth of jazz. He came north and was an influence on Bix Beiderbecke. He played with the New Orleans Rhythm Kings in Chicago for a while, and this is probably how George saw him, or it might be that George merely heard of him through Bix. Hardy had played in Bix's hometown of Davenport, Iowa. He died of TB in New Orleans.

56   Joseph "Wingy" Manone (1900-present) A New Orleans musician famous for his trumpet rather than cornet as George asserts. Manone lost his arm as a child in a streetcar accident in New Orleans. He has led several bands including the Cellar Boys and his song, *Tar Paper Stomp*, is believed to be the inspiration for Glenn Miller's *In the Mood*.

57   I have to assume George is speaking about Junior Mance, a percussionist who played with Wilbur Ware (1923-present), and was featured on Ware's album, *Chicago Sound*. Ware was, indeed, born in Chicago and has played with many of the greats including Art Blakey, Sonny Rollins, and Thelonious Monk.

58   Bebop is a style of jazz we tend to call "modern jazz" today. It started in the 40's—fast paced, innovative, with complex improvisation. Dizzy Gillespie, Charlie Parker , Thelonious Monk, and Art Tatum are among the leaders of the movement.

59   *Fidgety Feet* was recorded on March 10, 1924 at Gennett Records in Richmond, Indiana.

60   Bix Beiderbecke was dismissed in 1922 from the Lake Forest Academy, a boarding school in Lake Forest, Illinois, a far north suburb of Chicago. It appears drinking was the main culprit, but he was regularly sneaking out of his dorm to travel into Chicago to listen to jazz. During one of these excursions is no doubt when he met George. It was during this time that he famously wrote his brother, "I'd travel to hell to hear a good band."

61   Friar's Inn was located at 343 N. Wabash in Chicago and was one of the most famous jazz clubs/speakeasies of the 1920s. The band that made it famous was the New Orleans Rhythm Kings led by the cornetist Paul Mares, who had come north from New Orleans.

62   *That's a Plenty* is a Dixieland Jazz standard that was originally performed as a ragtime piece. The music was written in 1914 by Lew Pollack and was first recorded in 1917. The New Orleans Rhythm Kings also recorded it.

63   This is the only reference to a jazz band George allegedly led. George never mentions it again in the manuscript.

64   Billy Pierce (1927-present). Pierce was the White Sox' star pitcher from 1952-61. He was voted best American League pitcher in '56 and '57. He was a key part of the White Sox' World Series appearance in 1959.

65   Theodore Lyons (1900-present) pitched for the White Sox for 21 years and was inducted into the Hall of Fame in 1955. His best years were in the 1920s and '30s. It's interesting that George is confused about whether it was Billy Pierce or Ted Lyons he was watching. Their careers were decades apart. It also suggests George had some interest and awareness of baseball over a lot of years.

66   Johnny Dodds (1892-1940) Born in Mississippi, he became a professional clarinetist in New Orleans and died in Chicago. He played, as George comments, with Joseph "King" Oliver's Creole Jazz Band as well as with Jelly Roll Morton and Louis Armstrong. He was a major influence on Chicagoan Benny Goodman. He also worked with his younger brother and drummer, Warren "Baby" Dodds in their band, The New Orleans Bootblacks.

67   Johnny Weissmuller (1904-present) In contradiction to George, Johnny Weissmuller was not of Bohemian origin but had been born in the Austro-Hungarian Empire of which Bohemia was a part. Records indicate that Weissmuller was born near Timosoara in present-day Romania. Weissmuller attended Lane Tech High School in Chicago, so it is possible that George ran into him. It was in Chicago that Weissmuller's swimming talents came to the attention of a coach. Beside his movie role as Tarzan, Weissmuller competed in two Olympics in 1924 and 1928 and won five gold medals.

68   The Wolverines recorded some of the earliest and most famous recordings in the mid-1920s. *Fidgety Feet* was previously cited. Their wax pressings of *Copenhagen* and *Riverboat Shuffle* are legendary.

69   Beiderbecke was in St. Louis in 1925.

70   Jean Goldkette came to America in 1911 from France. His was probably the most famous jazz band in America in the late 1920s. Another jazz legend, Jimmy Dorsey, played with Beiderbecke in the band. Other jazz and swing legends were touched by that orchestra. The likes of Artie Shaw and Glenn Miller played sides with Goldkette.

71   Tommy Dorsey (1905-1956). Primarily a trombonist and one of the premier swing bandleaders, he was known as the "Sentimental Gentleman of Swing." It is likely George also ran into Tommy's brother, Jimmy, who was a powerhouse on his own as well as with the Goldkette orchestra.

72   Hoagy Carmichael (1899-present). Born in Bloomington, Indiana and trained at Indiana University, he was one of America's great songwriters. His appearance in the movie *To Have and Have Not* boosted his popularity. *Stardust*, *The Nearness of You* and *Georgia on My Mind* are among his most memorable compositions.

73   *Stardust*, written by Hoagy Carmichael in 1927 with lyrics added later by Michael Parrish, is an American standard. Hoagy Carmichael said that Bix Bedierbecke partly inspired the song. It became the sentimental ballad of George's reminiscence with more slowly recorded versions in 1930.

74   Miles Davis and Dizzy Gillespie

75   This is perhaps among the most difficult entries of the manuscript to reconcile. The Goldkette Orchestra did, indeed, travel to New York in 1926 to play at the Roseland Ballroom. It was there that the famous "Battle of the Bands" took place, where Goldkette was pitted against Fletcher Henderson's Negro band. The problem is I have no reason to believe Beiderbecke would have departed from Chicago. I assume they left from Detroit. A year or so earlier, The Wolverines traveled to New York, and they probably departed from Chicago. Sometime in this period Beiderbecke also joined the Whiteman Band, which was playing in New York at the time.

76   The Twentieth Century Limited is the New York Central's premier train, running from Chicago to the Grand Central Station in New York. The NYC has been running the train since 1902. I wonder if George knew his remark about the "red carpet treatment" originated with The Twentieth Century Limited. A red carpet is put out for its passengers at the stations, and it is from this practice the term was coined.

77   This is the correct date of Beiderbecke's death. I find it curious that George so often got facts and dates wrong in this manuscript, but had this date down cold.

78   George was likely referring to Old Grand Dad bourbon. I assume this episode occurred during prohibition, so was he speaking allegorically or was it some kind of illegally distilled liquor?

79   "El". George is using the idiomatic term for the elevated portions of Chicago's mass transit and subway system.

80   The New Deluxe Café was located at 3502 S. State St. and is most famously known for Jelly Roll Morton's performances there. Once again, it is difficult to sort out

the historical sequence of events. In the preceding section George comments about his birthday in 1925 or 26, but my research shows the New Deluxe Café being out of business by that time. There were many clubs nearby. The Elite Café mentioned earlier was at 3030 S. State. Interestingly, Milton "Mezz" Mezzrow mentions in his autobiography, *Really the Blues*, Random House 1946, on page 25, "The first place we dug was the DeLuxe Café at 35th and State....We had to wait outside in line because there was standing room only, but finally the headwaiter at the top of the stairs snapped his fingers and the doorman let us in." He goes on to mention listening to Alberta Hunter there. This certainly suggests to me that George was recounting a true experience. He apparently has the time out of sequence.

81   Milton "Mezz" Mezzrow: (1899-present). A jazz Clarinetist and saxophonist from Chicago who has spent most of his career in New York. He's known for his efforts at racially integrating bands. His recordings of Sidney Bechet are particularly famous.

82   Alberta Hunter (1895-present), came to Chicago from Memphis when she was twelve to sing the blues. She sang in a lot of the famous Chicago clubs, but then left the states in the late twenties for Paris, where she was a success. (Bechet also made a name for himself in Paris.) She was tireless in performing with the USO during the War both in Europe and the Pacific. It would seem, given Alberta's departure from America, that George may have confused times.

83   I've been unable to identify any recordings giving George credit.

84   At this time, a popular vacation destination for factory workers at the Western and other places around Cicero was the North Woods, which generally referred to the lake country in northern Wisconsin near Hayward or Rhinelander.

85   Riverview Amusement Park opened for business in 1904 and occupied 74 acres along the Chicago River at Western and Belmont.

86   Katherine's point is largely accurate but overly simplified. Many Czechs also went to Texas, Pennsylvania and numerous other states. In fact there was Czech immigration in the 18th century as well, some residing in New Amsterdam (New York) and Savannah, Georgia as examples. Moravians were among the first to arrive. Czech-Americans fought on both sides of the Civil War. In America's industrial expansion in the late 19th century, Chicago certainly was the hub of immigration. Czechs came to Chicago as early as the 1850s to work on the railroads. By the turn of the century, Chicago was the third largest Czech community in the world, behind Prague and Vienna.

87   My best estimate is this event must have taken place sometime between 1927-31. That would make George anywhere from 30 to 35.

88   *Just One of Those Things* was written by Cole Porter for the 1935 musical, *Jubilee*. It has been performed by all the greats and is considered an American standard.

89   George is quoting the opening lyrics of the 1926 Joseph "King" Oliver song, *Doctor Jazz*. It was famously recorded by Jelly Roll Morton.

90   George is no doubt referring to October 29, 1929. This was another day of drops in stock prices which began on "Black Tuesday", October 24th, ushering in the Great Depression.

91   *You Go to My Head*, a 1938 popular song written by J. Fred Coots, lyrics by Haven Gillespie. Recorded by most of the great jazz vocalists.

92   No doubt George is referring to the Duke Ellington song, *It Don't Mean a Thing (If It Ain't Got that Swing)*. Ellington wrote the music during breaks while playing at the Lincoln Tavern in Chicago in the summer of 1931. Lyrics were written by Irwin Mills. It has become a jazz standard and has come to symbolize the beginning of the swing era.

93   Zeke was obviously playing with the loss of love in his Valentine reference. Specifically, he was clearly referring to the February 14, 1929 mob execution by the Capone boys of seven members of the north side Irish gang run by Bugs Moran. The massacre occurred over the struggle for control of the city's illegal liquor sales. It made headline news across America.

94   There were 72,000 American gas casualties in WWI. More than 1,000 died from poison gas.

95   Hawthorne Park Race Track is located on Laramie in Cicero, quite close to George's house. The track opened in 1890 and was a popular racing venue all through the Depression.

96   The "Century of Progress", as the fair was named, was a money-making project that had over forty million visitors during its two year run. The first major league all-star game at Comiskey Park occurred in conjunction with the opening of the fair in 1933. The fair emphasized the theme of technology with many futuristic autos, science displays, and other machines.

97   Actually the quotation is a "War to end war", which was part of President Woodrow Wilson's declaration of war speech to Congress on April 2, 1917.

98   George is no doubt making reference to the fact that the town of Stickney in the 1920s and 30s was known for its Al Capone mob activity.

99   George is obviously referring to the widely popular song of the time, *Brother, Can You Spare a Dime*, written in 1932. It was part of the musical *New Americana*, and was used effectively by the FDR campaign for the Presidency in 1932.

100   William "Count" Basie (1904-present). A leading figure and bandleader of the swing era. While born in New Jersey with his earliest successes in New York, Basie was known as leader of the "Kansas City Sound."

101   The Pump Room is actually in the Ambassador East Hotel, not the Palmer House. Since the late 1930's, it has been Chicago's definition of swank, and a celebrity watering hole. It is mentioned in the song, *My Kind of Town* made famous by Frank Sinatra, and appeared in Hitchcock's *North by Northwest*.

102   Tommy Dorsey (1905-56) Jazz trombonist and bandleader known as the "Sentimental Gentleman of Swing". Dorsey would have met Bix Beiderbecke while playing with the Whiteman band. This perhaps is where George recalled this statement.

103   Pullman is an area of Chicago from roughly 106th to 115th streets south and Cottage Grove on the west. It was the location of the planned utopian industrial community built in the 1880s by the railroad car manufacturer, George Pullman. His sleeper cars were named after him. In the great economic contraction of 1893, Pullman reduced workers' wages and laid off many. Rents in his corporate subsidized housing, however, remained the same, and this was the precipitating cause of a labor walkout. Pullman refused arbitration, and the subsequent strike crippled the American railroad industry. There was considerable violence and federal troops were brought in to restore order.

104   Benjamin "Benny" Goodman (1909- present). Known as the "King of Swing". A clarinetist and highly successful bandleader whose concert in Carnegie Hall in New York was met with critical acclaim, giving jazz respectability. Goodman was born in Chicago of Jewish parents.

105   Johnny Dodds (1892-1940). A New Orleans clarinetist and major influence on Benny Goodman. Dodds performed frequently in Chicago during the 20s, so George could have heard him at a number of places. Dodds played with Jelly Roll Morton's Red Hot Peppers and Louis Armstrong's Hot 5 band.

106   *Stormy Weather* (1933) was written by Harold Arlen and Ted Koehler. Lena Horne made one of the first recordings of the song, but it became a standard. Billie Holiday's recording is also noteworthy. The part of the line George left out is, "Ever since my gal and I ain't together." My best guess is George was just trying to make the lyrics fit his mood, and the reference to a relationship simply didn't match his intention.

107   "Doughboy" was a popular nickname for U.S. soldiers in WWI. I am not sure of the origin of the term, but it was used in the 19th century.

108   *Over There* was written by George M. Cohan in 1917 and instantly became a rallying song, igniting patriotic fervor in WWI and again in WWII. The chorus goes:

> "Over there, over there
> Send the word, send the word over there
> That the Yanks are coming, the Yanks are coming
> The drum are rum-tumming everywhere.
> So prepare, say a prayer,
> Send the word, send the word to beware
> *We'll be over, we're coming over,*
> *And we won't come back til' it's over over there"*

109   Phosgene gas was used extensively in WWI, and by the Japanese against the Chinese. It is a choking agent and works by irritating and damaging the lining of the lung and potentially causing dry-land drowning.

110   George is in the ballpark. Actually, the 21st Amendment ending prohibition was passed in 1933.

111   George is clearly referring to the popular 1939 song by Rube Bloom with lyrics by Johnny Mercer, *Day In and Day Out*.

112   No doubt a reference to another 1939 song, *Darn that Dream,* which first appeared in the Broadway musical, *Swingin' the Dream*, written by Jimmy Van Heusen with lyrics by Eddie DeLange. Now a jazz standard performed by many of the greats. to include: Benny Goodman, Tommy Dorsey, Miles Davis, Thelonious Monk to name a few.

113   George's confusing historical recitation likely refers to the Marco Polo Bridge incident on July 7, 1937, which is generally viewed as the opening of full-blown hostilities between Imperial Japan and China.

114   George has created legend out of another legend. Americans associate Marco Polo with the importation of pasta to Europe from China in 1295. There is no evidence that Marco Polo invented spaghetti.

115   This conclusion also appears simplistic. The U.S. military and other aid to China was indeed growing at the time, but it wasn't until after Pearl Harbor in 1941, that the pace skyrocketed. What George is likely observing about factory activity in Chicago was a nudging of the economy toward expansion for war.

116   A worker who replaces a striking worker. Someone who crosses a union picket line to work.

117   The Bobbsey Twins children's book series began in 1904 and is still popular. Bert and Nan are twin brother and sister. George has never made any literary allusions before. It was popular idiomatic expression at that time to call people the Bobbsey twins if you meant something slightly derisive but also comical and a little bit tongue-in-cheek.

118   Benjamin Francis Webster (1909-present). An influential tenor saxophonist who played with many major jazz bands in the 1930s and has recorded solo as well. He has been nicknamed "The Brute" and was influenced by the early jazz saxophonist Johnny Hodges.

119   I am going to suggest George must be referring to Claude Debussy's *Danses Sacree Et Profane,* which Debussy wrote on commission in 1904 for the Pleyel musical instrument company. Debussy said it was inspired, in part, by his Portuguese friend and pianist, Francisco de Lacerda.

120   This is a reference to Adolf Hitler, made popular at the time particularly in Chicago following a speech on May 18, 1937 by Chicago's Cardinal George Mundelein who said, of Hitler, "Perhaps you will ask how it is a nation of 60 million people will submit in fear and servitude to an alien, an Austrian paper-hanger, and a poor one at that."

121   British Prime Minister Lloyd George is associated with the 1919 post WWI treaty negotiations in Paris, which in fact allowed for the creation of an independent Czechoslovakia after the collapse of the Austro-Hungarian Empire. George certainly means to say British Prime Minister Neville Chamberlain, who along with the French acquiesced to or attempted to "appease" Germany over territorial claims in the Sudetenland to avert war which, in effect, opened the door for German annexation of Czechoslovakia. The Munich agreement is famously waved before the cameras by Chamberlain, who declares in London, "Peace for our Time."

122   In saying Bohemia was sold down the river he is referring to the idiom which refers to the practice in the early 1800s in which rich homeowners sold unwanted servants into slavery, sending them down the Mississippi River to plantations in the south.

123   Edvard Benesh (1884-1948). A leader of the Czech independence movement and noted pre-war diplomat. He was the president of Czechoslovakia at the time of the September 29, 1938 Munich Agreement, opening up annexation by Germany. Benesh led the Czech government in exile from Britain form 1940-45. He refused to sign the post-WWII communist Constitution and died shortly thereafter.

124   Boys in the trenches refers to WWI.

125   Victory gardens sprang up as part of the war effort to take the strain off of food shortages. People were encouraged to grow locally in yards and parks.

126   By my calculations, George was between 42 and 45 on December 7, 1941.

127   *Davenport Blues* was recorded on January 26, 1925 in Richmond, Indiana. On the flip side was *Toddlin' Blues*. *Davenport Blues* was an original composition of Beiderbecke. Davenport, as you may recall, was Beiderbecke's home town.

128   I debated writing this note because I didn't want to break up George's narrative with an academic definition, but then I thought it might be a useful "syncopation" to provide it as a means to appreciate George's commentary. I wish to thank Chuck Shelton, my newspaper's music critic, for the technical aspects of this definition. Bebop grew out of the Swing era and is characterized by smaller musical groups. It tends to use a chromatic twelve-note scale with a lot of improvisation and intellectually challenging melodies and chord structures. There are a lot of attempts to say where the term "Bebop" originated, but the most convincing for me is that it represents the staccato two-tone phrase of this jazz form. Whereas Swing was primarily dance music, Bebop is to be listened to. It started to emerge in the mid-forties, but it really came into form in the last decade, so it's generally what we call "modern jazz." I consider one of the gifts George gave me was to introduce me through his manuscript to Bebop.

129   Clark Terry (1920-present). A Swing and Bop trumpeter who pioneered the flugelhorn in jazz. He played in the Count Basie and Duke Ellington bands, among others.

130   Invented in the early 19th century, the Fluegelhorn has a wider bell and different mouthpiece than a trumpet. It makes a fatter tone. It is generally considered to have a sound between a cornet and trumpet.

131   John Birks "Dizzy" Gillespie (1917-present). Along with Charlie Parker and Thelonius Monk is considered a key figure in the development of Bebop. In the early fifties Parker began playing with a trumpet with the bell pointed up at a 45 degree angle, and it became, along with his puff-cheeked style of play, his trademark.

132   *Night in Tunisia*, a 1942 song written by Gillespie that is one of his signature pieces and a jazz standard performed by jazz instrumentalists and vocalists alike.

133   First earth-orbiting satellite launched by the Soviet Union on October 4, 1957.

134   Maxwell "Max" Roach (1924-present). On the short list of Bebop greats.

135   Minton's Playhouse is a jazz club at 210 West 118th St. in Harlem. It was founded in the late thirties and was made famous as the place where the Bebop artists like Parker performed.

136   George is surely referring to the Juilliard School for the Fine Arts in New York.

137   Bird is a nickname for Charlie Parker.

138   No doubt George means diverticulosis.

139   At this point in the original manuscript George inserted a drawing of a mushroom cloud.

140   The Prudential Building is the tallest building in Chicago at 41 stories. It was completed in 1955, so we can date George's reflections about notes to sometime after 1955. We can estimate his age at this point to be approximately 55-60.

141   The Thaya River runs for about 140 miles in central Europe, at times forming the border with Austria. Certainly it is in the area of the Austrian Border where Karel apparently swam across.

142   The song refers to Louis Armstrong singing *Basin Street Blues.*

> *"Won't you come and go with me*
> *Down that Mississippi*
> *We'll take a boat to the land of dreams*
> *Come along with me on down to New Orleans*
> *Now the band's there to greet us*
> *Old friends will meet us.*
> *Where all them folks going to St, Louis cemetery meet*
> *Heaven on earth. . . they call it Basin Street."*

143   Elysium Fields is in fact a street in New Orleans. The name comes from Greek mythology, meaning a resting place in the afterlife for the heroic and virtuous. It's mentioned by Homer in *The Odyssey,* and Virgil as well. Recently Tennessee Williams refers to the New Orleans neighborhood of the Elysium Fields in the play and movie *A Streetcar Named Desire.*

About the Author

Philip T. Nemec

Philip T. Nemec grew up in the Chicago area and has been writing all his life. He currently lives in the Washington, DC area with his wife and two college age children.

CPSIA information can be obtained at www.ICGtesting.com
Printed in the USA
BVOW03*1756300614

357642BV00002B/6/P